FOU by Angel Williams & Judith Jackson

I0671896

Fou

Until death do us part

FOU by Angel Williams & Judith Jackson

Star City Publications

P.O Box 7322

Harrisburg, Pa 17113

www.starcitypublications.com

ISBN- 13: 9780692492703

ISBN- 10: 0692492704

First printing 2015

Printed in the United States of America

20 1 1 9 0 2 7 4 0

This is a work of fiction. Any references or similarities to actual events, real people, living, or dead, or to actual locales are intended to give the novel a sense of reality. Any similarity in other names, characters, places, and incidents is entirely coincidental.

Acknowledgments- Angel Williams

First and foremost I want to give thanks, praise, and glory to the man above. Without my God, none of this would have been possible! God has been truly blessing me and I will always remain humble and thankful for my blessings. I have been so blessed with the amazing gift of writing, always and forever all thanks and glory to God!

Kady Baby (Kaydence Miracle-Marie Gwynn) Once you discover your great talents. The gifts that God blesses you with, you will drop Kaydence and famously be known as "Thee Miracle-Marie" lol yes I have high standards for you. All the late nights and the long hours of non-stop writing is for you, my precious baby. You are my motivation and my inspiration. It's because of you I push even harder and work even harder. I love you with all my heart, you are my world!

I would like to thank my mommy, Brenda Williams, who has always been here for me no matter what. She's always supporting me in any type of way shape or form that she can. My strong will come from her. Mom thanks for molding me to be the woman that I am. Love you.

My brothers and sisters, Joy Williams, James Williams JR., Erica Williams thank you so much for always supporting me and reading my books and spreading the words. It's nothing like having family that always has your back!

Eric Gwynn Thank you for pushing me and motivating me all the time! If you see me not writing you get on me and never allow me to give up! My better half you are all that I need, you totally complete me! Seven long years and we are still going and strong as ever!

Jamie Glover, thank you for always be a supportive friend!

In the past year or so I've have met some amazing people and since the day I've met them they have been supporting me unconditionally. Thank you so much, Karen Williams and Tina Nance. I'm grateful to have met you all!!

Judi, I'm so glad that I met you. I learned so much from you. You are a kind-hearted person, an amazing person with a good heart! I love you and I'm honored to work on this amazing project with you!

To my lovely readers you guys totally rock! I can't name you all, but it's some that I want to give a special thanks to who have been supporting me since day one, without you guys I wouldn't be Thee Author Angel Williams. ☺ I'm so grateful to have you guys as readers! Your word of encouragement is what keeps me going and going and going!!

To my family, who has supported me, thank you so much. Aunt Carolyn, Uncle Eddie, Zack, Antwan, Aunt

Doris, Uncle Double T, Javita, Jordan, Man Man, Baby D, Sarah Ann, Ashleigh Zupanovic, Lawanda McDonald, Aunt Tina F., I love you guys!

I won't even take the time to acknowledge my haters, just know that I have too much faith in God and to many supporters for you to stop me! ☺

To anyone who is inspired by my writing and my motivation and you are an aspiring author, just keep pushing, keep on writing. Don't stop until you are satisfied. Put hard work into what you do and love what you do. Hard work and dedication are the KEYS TO SUCCESS!

To anyone who I forgot, you are always special to me and I'm grateful for having you in my life!

_____ Please put your name here.

Connect with on Facebook and Instagram Author Angel Williams (angeltherealdeal) and Twitter Star City Writer.

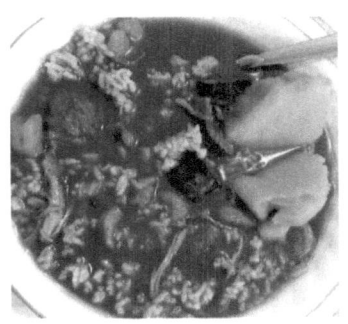

Acknowledgments- Judith Jackson

I would like to send many hugs and kisses to first and foremost my fans. Without you believing in my dreams, I wouldn't have as much drive as I do. Thank you to Angel Williams for helping me make my vision come to life with this masterpiece, you are amazing. Thank you to the publishers, and the editors who took the time to help make this a reality. Thank you to God, and the universe, which placed me in the position to be able to make my dreams come true. Thank you to my family for supporting me throughout all my craziness. Thank you to anyone who never doubted me. And most of all, I want to thank my parents. You all have instilled into me wits, determination, a hard work ethic, and entrepreneurship skills. You also gave me life. I would not be here if it weren't for you. I will always respect you, and honor you, and cherish you even if it's not in the physical. I love you....

I know I am a princess because a queen and a king raised me. You spent your life working to make sure I wouldn't need for anything, and I didn't. There was not a Christmas that I didn't have tons of presents under the tree, an Easter that I didn't have a basket full of candy, or a Halloween that I didn't go trick-or-treating, even when it was raining and you all had to drive me from house to house. Although our time was cut short, the memories and what you have instilled in me will last a lifetime. Mommy, you were a boss, and the most beautiful woman in the world (I know that will never change, even in your next life). Manager of a purchasing department in a hospital, to being a commissioner of the state of Illinois, a part of the human rights committee. Daddy, you were partners with Hennessy and Johnny Walker Red. You even went on to open up your own trucking company, WEJAC, INC. A part of the racing board. You were a veteran and fought for your country. You also fought for your family. That's only some of all the great things you both did, besides being my backbone.

I had the greatest childhood, and 25 years filled with love from you all. With all you have taught me and showed me, I have no choice but to be successful, and a boss like you all. I have gained knowledge and discipline through you. Although you all aren't here physically, I know you are here spiritually. I could not have asked for better parents. I dedicate not only this book to you but also my life. I know I have two guardian angels lighting my way. I love you both. Forever and always, even now that death has done us part... Only for now, because I know I will see you in the afterlife. - Love always, Judi

In loving memory and celebrating the life of

William E. Jackson Sr. & Girvena M. LeBlanc

Dress from Adore My Couture (Shatoya Malveaux-owner)

Shot by Karl Ray of karlrayphoyography.com, hair and makeup by Lanetra Herring

Accessories by Girvena LeBlanc

Everyday to Someday

I wake up every morning,
and see the crystal dew,
Wishing that my dreams,
Were unbelievably true.

That you were still here,
To help me through the day,
And give me unconditional love,
Like you had done every day.

The smell of breakfast cooking,
The sound of cutting grass,
The Cadillac pulling in the driveway,
Catching lightning bugs and putting them in jars of glass.

Running through the sprinklers in the summer,
The home cooked dinners so well prepared,
The strong hands that wrapped birthday gifts,
The memories that we shared.

The arguments we had,
We ended them with laughter,
And every time I dropped a tear,
You had a hug to give me after.

The road trips down south,
Trying food in every state,
Seeing the sun rise and set,
It must have been our fate.

I try not to be cold and bitter,
and I try not to be mad,
Because I know I will see you in the afterlife,
my beautiful parents, mom and dad.

And when we do reunite,
The pain will be gone,
It will be like we never left each other,
And our love and destiny together will continue on strong.

– Judith C. Jackson

Connect with the Authors

Angel Williams

Facebook: Author Angel Williams

Twitter: Starcitywriter

Instagram: Angeltherealdeal or Author Angel Williams

Judith Camille Jackson

Facebook: www.facebook.com/officialjudijai

Twitter: JudiJaiKrazi

Instagram: MissJudiJai

Website: www.sojudijai.com

To all our loyal #dawls and fans! We appreciate your love and ongoing support! Thank you so much! ☺ And for all the people fighting for their life, fighting for their breath, fighting for their peace and happiness, fighting for their strength, fighting for their pain to go away, fighting for their loved ones, fighting for themselves, fighting for a cure… this is for you. #FuckCancer.

Angel Williams was born in Harrisburg, Pennsylvania. She was raised in a loving family of five children, and a best friend who she'll always call her sister, who has been with her through many of her journeys. She has an amazing, God fearing mother who always pushed her to do her best, a terrific father, the late James Terry Williams Sr. RIP, who also pushed her to do the best she could do, and taught her morals and values, and to be positive. A great little sister, Joy Williams, who always looked up to her, and the best brother, James Williams, anyone could ask for. He always expects the best out of her, and he is a man who will always give anyone his last!

Angel's love for writing developed while she attended Dauphin County Technical School. In 2001, she suffered a tragic loss, which ignited her passion for writing poetry and short stories. She often shared her writing with family and friends, who encouraged her to get her work published and become an author. She always dreamed of becoming an author, but she was too overwhelmed with life. Angel graduated in 2004 and was so tired of living in a small town; she wanted more out of life. She needed to be in a place with more opportunities, so she decided to take on a big city and moved to Baltimore, Maryland, where she currently resides with her precious baby girl Kaydence Miracle-Marie. Her daughter means the world to her and always gives her the motivation that she needs.

She is an aunt to three; Amazing Jayvan Garcia, Alexis, Javita, Jordan, James Jr., De'mani Williams & Kerry & Kiara Harris. Angel is a loving sister to Joy & James Williams & Erica. Angel love to spend her spare time writing, shopping (a big stress reliever), promoting events, crabbing, traveling, and spending time with the ones she loves. She loves to give back to her community in any way she can.

With strong encouragement from her family and friends, she finally got the push she needed to get her first novel Envy: The Root Of All Evil published. Angel Williams is now one of Baltimore's Best Selling Authors of Envy The Root Of All Evil 1 & 2 &3, Raven's Cravings- A Baltimore Tale, Pretty Money, Momma I Ain't No SAINT, Gold Diggin Honeys and many more titles. Over the years, Angel has developed an incredible fan base, who all believed that Raven's Cravings should be a motion picture. In 2010, Angel wrote the script to Raven's Cravings based on the book. Titled it. Raven's Cravings – A Bmore Love Thing. She and her readers felt like Raven story was a must read, and should be read throughout the world. Raven story was very story and powerful and had a great impact on others. Now the incredible story is a must see, in which thousands of readers are patiently waiting to see on the "Big Screen."

In 2011, Angel decided to branch off on her own and start her own publishing company. She is now the proud founder and CEO of Star City Publications "Where dreams come true." She started this publishing company in hopes to help other aspiring authors get published. As of today, her publishing company has over ten great novels published. Her company is standing tall and is very successful.

So far in her life, she has been very blessed and now she just wants to be successful & continue living her dreams.

Words from Angel Williams "Dream BIG, dream all you can dream. Because dreams do come true. I'm living proof. Putting God first. Hard work, dedication, determination, motivation all dreams are possible."

"The greatest moments are when people tell me that I inspire them. I want to be an inspiration for everyone to do all they can do. For them to know it's possible to come from the bottom and make way to the top."

Judith Camille Jackson was born a Pisces on March 8, 1989. Raised in the south suburbs of Chicago, with roots from Lake Charles, Louisiana, she got the best of both worlds; the city lights and the country sunsets. Her mother, Girvena LeBlanc was born and raised in Louisiana as a full Louisiana Creole. Her father, William Jackson, was born an African American in Tennessee and raised in Chicago. Judith aka Judi, was raised as an only child and her parents always made sure she stayed active. From ballet, tap, and jazz, to piano, to art classes like pottery, drawing and painting, to her always listening to music and writing poems and raps, Judi was destined to be a star. Her mother always recorded on home videos whatever she did, because she was always a very entertaining and energetic child.

In middle school and high school, Judi was a cheerleader, played volleyball, basketball, was very active in the school newspaper and was also a student ambassador. It was then she realized she didn't only like to be the center of attention, but she also liked working behind the scenes to create. She went on to pursue her love of the arts at Columbia College Chicago, one of the biggest media arts schools in the country, to study Broadcast Journalism Radio and Television. Her junior year, with a stroke of fate and destiny, she was cast for the 7th season of Oxygen Network's hit series "The Bad Girls Club," which ironically happened to take place in New Orleans, and Judi took over the whole show. It was history from that moment forward. She got every spin-off, winning a love competition show, hosted specials, one in which she also won the title of "The Funniest Bad Girl Of All Time."

FOU by Angel Williams & Judith Jackson

Judi always had a mysterious, mystical and magical imagination, which was enhanced by her love of being Creole, and her love of being creative. She loves the unknown, the spiritual world and loves animals and nature more than anything (besides good ole southern cookin').

Judi realizes the influence of technology and media, and she is looking forward to making a change, not only within her but within others too.

All of our lovely supporters, thank you so much! To list some…

Nette Gilliam

Destiny Tillman

Nyi-Trell TyShawn Bean

Deshaun Summers

Michael DeFellipo

Rashone Evans

Jalissa Davis

Matthew Navarrete

Intro

I always knew I was different. Not only because of the fact that I was "yellow," or had dark brown curly hair which refused to stay in the bun my mama used to style my hair in on those hot summer days. No matter how many times I tried to slick down the annoying little frizzy hairs, they would just never slick down. They would rest wildly over the top of my head, the same dark color until the summer hit and lightened my hair to auburn red.

Papa and I sat on the front porch as I sipped my iced tea. I looked over at him as he peacefully rocked back and forward in his rocking chair. Sticking my tongue out, I licked the water condensing on the outside of the glass jar as the ice melted, watering down my sweet tea. Papa told me to hurry up and drink it before the wasps smelled the sugar and came to sting me. Papa was always right. Those darn wasps always stung me. I should've drunk it faster. My perfect bun and a perfect jar of sweet tea weren't the only things that wouldn't stay. Something was different about me, perhaps strange …

My name is Summer, and that's pretty strange, or should I say ironic since I was born on the coldest winter night Louisiana ever experienced in '92.

It was the worst snowstorm in Louisiana's history. Actually, it was the only snowstorm Louisiana had ever experienced. My mama said as soon as her water broke, she got dressed and was ready to step outside the door until she realized that she was snowed in. She called upstairs to my papa, who rushed downstairs. After seeing all the snow, he informed her to call 911.

Three and a half hours later, I was born into the world on my papa's living room floor. Mama birthed a hazel-green eyed, unique baby with a sunny smile on what seemed like the coldest night ever. Nobody knew if I was Spanish, Black, mixed, or even white, until I got a little older and would tell everybody... I'm Creole.

I'll never forget that time I went crawfishing with my friend, Abby, and her mama. I was so happy because Papa never let me go anywhere. It was always just the two of us after the loss of my dear mama. Abby and her mama lived not too far from us on Sea Street. We had been friends for over eight years. I was 14 years old and she was 15 years old. I couldn't wait to catch some big ole crawfishes to bring back to Papa. Making sure he was happy was what I always did. I loved to see a smile painted on his handsome face.

We had been out all day, and we hardly caught anything. I started to cry. Upset that I wasn't going to be able to make Papa smile, I wanted to give up, but my determination wouldn't allow me to do so. Abby and her mama told me to stop crying. I wasn't paying them any mind. I had my own agenda, one that they probably wouldn't understand. Abby had everything in the world, including her mama, and sometimes she just didn't understand me....

My tears immediately dried up when I saw something over by the moss trees, not far from the mud we were getting crawfish from. I squinted, and it seemed as if my eyes were playing tricks on me.

"I caught another one, Mama!" Abby screamed.

I glared at the big crawfish that she had just caught. A bit envious, I must admit.

With tears in my eyes yet again, I stared down at my shoes. My shoes were wet, and the sun had started to set, making the sky a grapefruit color so red you would think it was bleeding love... I stared at the tree, and yet again, I thought I saw something. Maybe I was just hot and bothered. Or maybe I didn't see anything at all. I wiped my eyes. Grabbing a stick, I began playing in the mud, waiting for my something to bite my line. There was no way I was going to go home without bringing back any crawfish for Papa.

Hopelessly waiting, I felt myself getting angrier and angrier about not catchin' one dag on crawfish for Papa. I stared at Abby, who was walking over to me.

"Summer, you look funny. You are very pale, you just don't seem like yourself," she told me.

I stared at the front side of my hands and noticed the paleness instead of the high yellow complexion my skin normally was. *GOOD*! I thought to myself. I was tired of being called yellow, and red. Now I was pale.

"I HOPE ALL THESE CRAWFISH DIE!" I yelled as I jumped to my feet. "I WISH ALL THESE CRAWFISH WOULD JUST DIE!" I repeated with my fist balled up.

Abby and her mama got real quiet, a strange look crept onto their faces. As if they were frightened. Maybe my outrage shocked them a bit. At first I didn't know why, until I turned around and every crawfish in the field rose above the muddy water to catch the last bit of sunlight that God would grant us on that spring day. They weren't moving at all. It was apparent that they were dead.

I got really excited and jumped up and down. I ran over to grab a few crawfishes. I couldn't wait to take the fishes back to Papa and to tell him what I had done. He always told me that I was some sort of special. Now I understood what he meant.

"I got some crawfishes," I yelled to Abby.

When I turned around, I realized Abby was dead too. She was pale, and her face was frozen in an awkward smile. Her mama started going crazy. Started calling me a witch, calling me a voodoo queen. Saying I killed her daughter and the crawfish with black magic. The hurtful phrases hit me like punches.

"NO! NO! NO!" I cried. "I JUST WANTED THE CRAWFISH DEAD!" I yelled in my defense.

All I wanted was the crawfish dead, not my best friend. My only friend.

Abby's mama ran toward me and tried to hit me. She missed and knocked me into the swamp. She didn't stop.

"I LOVED ABBY! I WOULDN'T WANT HER DEAD!" I screamed.

Abby's mama didn't care. She swung at me again.

This time, defending myself, I grabbed her by her head, pulling some of her hair out. She grabbed a big branch off the moss tree and tried to knock the daylights out of me. It was evident that she was tryin' to kill me. Just when she went to swing at me, her arms stopped in mid-air, holding the thick branch up with no strain. She looked scared, frozen. Not even looking at me, her stare was focused behind me.

I turned around, and that's when I saw it. The thing I had seen earlier. It was a shadow. My shadow. I couldn't understand how I had seen my own shadow by the trees earlier, or how I saw my own shadow after sunset ...

My papa was happy when I got home. He wondered how I got so much crawfish. After we had boiled them, I went into the bathroom and looked in the mirror. I was yellow again. Thinking about Abby and her mama, tears began to run down my face. I was human and only wanted to be normal. I hurt just like another one would. The only difference about me was that I was some sort of special. Getting ready for a shower, I took off my overalls, and inside my pocket was the hair I had accidentally pulled out of Abby's mama's head. I didn't even realize it. Deciding to keep it, I eased it back in my pocket. I loved Abby and her mama.

Abby and her mama's bodies were never found. Soon, I realized the things that I loved would never stay. No matter how *hard* I tried...

Chapter 1

Abella

I was born in a small town called Cap-Haitian, a northern coastal port and the capital of the Department of Nord in Haiti. It's a beautiful place, known for its architecture and artistic ways. I never knew my father. All I know of him is he worked on the gingerbread houses that lined the street. My mother used to joke all the time and say she killed him in his dream. The only picture I had of him was taken on his deathbed, and that was all. It was pathetic. I didn't even have memories of him. Never even wanted to think of him, I had no reason to do so.

Kreyol was my first language. My family and I learned English from tourists who visited the island, and by reading a lot. My family was a part of the better off crowd in Haiti. We had our times like all the islanders, though. My mom made good money cooking for locals. From time to time, she would work at the hotels as a bartender. That job made a lot of money from all the tourists. Despite Haiti's dark and poor reputation, we got many travelers. I went to private school, Union, while living on the island. We all wore white collared cotton shirts with navy bottoms. Skirts for the girls with knee high cotton socks and long pants for the boys, no matter how hot it was. I played volleyball for the most part, and in my spare time, I made beaded-feather jewelry and sold them from my backpack. You could call me the Haitian Hustler.

Everyone on the island knew each other. My mom used to take my brothers and me under the grotto ceiling to rituals and ceremonies for the iwa and loas (voodoo spirits). That's where I learned how to dance so well. I'll never forget the first time I saw my mom sacrifice a black pig. We sat there in pigs' blood for hours until all the spirits were contacted and they came into our dimension. Every time someone on the island died, we would have a ceremony for the soul of the person crossing over.

My mother was very strict on our Haitian roots and education. The first time I tried voodoo was November 1, during Fet Gede when I was seven years old. This light skinned Haitian named Nanah used to mess with me in school. She would always put lizards in my desk and sand in my backpack to make it heavy. She felt like she was above darker complexions just because her mother was French and she had married a Cuban ambassador. Her hair was down to her waist, and the only reason she still lived on the island was because of the scenery and the Cuban cigar shop her family owned here.

I was fed up. I took my nail file and cut a lock of her hair one day when I was standing in line behind her waiting to drink from the water fountain. It was so long, she didn't even realize it. When I got home that afternoon, I chewed five packs of bubble gum and stuck every piece into the lock of hair. I promised myself I would only kill an animal one time and one time only, and that was for this spell. I went to my back yard and grabbed a chicken.

It was making noises out of terror, so I quickly stabbed it with my nail file. All I needed was the blood. I mixed it in with the furry ball of bubble gum and set it on fire. It was still daytime, so no one saw flames. I stomped the fire out after I spit on it three times. I then buried the remains under the well near my house.

The next day, Nanah fell asleep at her desk with a mouth full of gum. When she woke up, all her beautiful long hair was stuck in her mouth, intertwined with the wad of mango bubble gum she had been chewing. She screamed. It took the teacher two hours to cut all the gum out of her hair. It left her pretty much bald. She didn't show up to school the next day. Many thought she was too embarrassed to come back, until news spread around the island that her father had fallen asleep while smoking one of his own Cuban cigars. Their whole house caught on fire. Nanah's parents burned to death, while she escaped from the house, blinded by ashes and smoke, screaming in pain from her burnt flesh. She fell into her watery grave in a well by her house.

I was a loner. I spent my time reading and mixing ingredients for cooking or the healing rituals the island held for the elderly. My mother always warned us to never try to play the role of God though, and I didn't until I got older and lost my mother and my two brothers.

My two brothers, Alain and Valery passed away within days of each other from Malaria and yellow fever. Shortly after my brothers' deaths, my mother fell ill, due to mold in our attic and died. I almost passed as well, but because my body was younger and healthier, I survived.

After my mother's death, I was sent to New Orleans to live with my mother's sister, Adias. Her daughter,

Abella, was three years younger, and we formed an instant bond. Living in America was a difficult adjustment. Our family was locally despised for our special gifts, and I didn't fit in at all. In fact, I was a favorite target for ridicule and bullying. If it wasn't for Summer, I'm sure I would've destroyed the town by now.

Summer was my best friend. She and I understood each other to the max. We were like sisters from another mother. Some even said that we favored each other a bit, with the same sort of wild and curly hair. The two of us had so many similarities it was fou. She didn't know her mama, nor did I. Well, it wasn't that I didn't know my mama. I knew her, but when she passed, I refused to speak much of her. That didn't stop me from thinking about her at times.

Summer was born in Louisiana, but we both were Creole, and to make matters even better, we both were some sorts of special. Born with a special gift, that only the two of us understood. That's why from day one we clicked and had been best friends ever since. It was like the two of us were meant to be together until death do us part…

From the day we met, everything between us had become great memories and history in the making.

I had run out of the classroom, leaving a trail of laughter behind me and rushed into the girls' bathroom. I burst through the stall, and threw the toilet seat down with a swift kick. My weary body flopped down on the seat and I buried my face into my hands, allowing the tears to escape. A few stalls down, I heard a door being kicked open.

Hearing the kicks getting closer, I grabbed my belongings and stood on top of the toilet. I didn't know if someone was coming after me or what.

"Where are you?" I heard a voice say.

On my tippy toes, I stood and saw the curly locks flowing wildly.

Summer was a girl in my class, and we'd only started speaking a few days ago. I had seen her around in the past, we just never really hung out or anything of that sort. We would say our hi's and bye's and that was about it. Why was she looking for me? Did I do something wrong to her?"

She stood in front of my stall and sent a powerful kick to the door, flinging it wide open.

I jumped and gripped my belongings even tighter.

"Why you look so scared?" She questioned with her hands on her hips.

"I'm not scared!" I shook my head.

"Then why are you hiding?" she asked, pulling her hair out of her face.

I stared at her cherubic face and shrugged. "I'm not hiding, nor am I scared."

She shook her head; her curls flowed all over the place. "I'm not hiding, nor am I scared," she said in a baby voice, mocking me.

I turned my nose up at her and was about to say something until she reached her hands out.

"Do you wanna face the music together?" she asked with a smile.

I grabbed her hand and jumped down from the toilet. when I felt how cold her hand was, I snatched my hand back. I thought I was the only one with ice-cold hands.

"I'm always cold." She laughed and grabbedmy hand again.

We walked together, hand in hand, back to our classroom.

"No more dealing with that bully stuff. We are in 11th grade now. We are grown women, we can't continue to be bullied," Summer advised me.

I nodded. She was right. There was no way I was going to continue to be bullied, especially allowing it to go on my entire life. I never bothered anyone, yet everyone wanted to bother me. Usually, I just ignored the taunts and whispers, but that day, it was all too much. After what I'd been through, it was just too much …

It all started when I had hung out with Wallace a few nights prior.

I should have known he was way out of my league. Him sending me love letters for three weeks straight, always at my locker after each period didn't do my craving for his love any justice. The fact that he was one of the cool kids on the block and he was super fine did nothing but stroke my ego. So, when he invited me to the party, I thought nothing of it. Only that he liked me enough to be seen with me in public. I was far from ugly, actually I thought I was gorgeous. It was just that I didn't get invited to any outside of school events.

That night, in particular, I took an extra hour getting dressed. I snuck into my cousin Adele's room and grabbed her shortest and tightest skirt. I also borrowed her makeup and a pair of diamond studded wedges. I took my time brushing my wild curls, perfectly containing them. Once they under control, I put a lot of water and moose on them. I couldn't believe all it took was a little time for my curls to look so beautiful.

I painted my face with makeup to perfection.

Looking at myself in the tall mirror, I damn near cried. I couldn't believe how gorgeous I looked. All it took was a little time and patience for me to enhance my beauty.

"Where are you going, dressed like that?" Adele asked as she burst into my room, "And is that my makeup and my skirt? Damn, are those my shoes too?" Adele asked.

I nodded my head yes. "I'm going out with Wallace to a party," I bragged, wearing a broad smile.

"Wallace? You better be careful hanging with him. I heard so many rumors about him," Adele warned. "And you better not have my panties on too." She sneered as she left my room.

I shrugged. At the honk of Wallace's horn, I grabbed my purse and raced outside.

"And you look so pretty," I heard Adele yell after me.

When I got in the car, I literally had to grab Wallace's jaw before it dropped on the floor. He was drooling and all.

"Wow, Abella." He gasped. "I didn't know how beautiful you were, and damnnnn girl, look at your body."

I covered my mouth as I giggled like a little girl. My cheeks were flushed with redness and I couldn't stop the blushing.

"Let's go for ice cream and then to the movies," Wallace suggested.

"No! I want to go to that party." I whined.

Wallace and I debated whether we were going to the party or out for ice cream and to the movies.

As always, I got my way. Fifteen minutes later, we pulled up to the party. It was obvious that I was feeling myself, not that I felt myself too often. Wallace rushed over to the passenger door and opened it for me. He was such a gentleman.

He reached for my hand, and I gave it to him and smiled. "You are so sweet," I told him, walking behind him as he led the way into the party.

Females were all half-naked, and the majority of them were drunk, as they danced and pranced around everywhere.

It was awkward when I got the uneasy looks from females. I could literally hear the rude whispers from all directions as females called me all sorts of horrible names. I've never done anything to anyone. I didn't understand why people didn't like me, and I was tired of hearing all that damn because I'm different and I'm special crap! What did I do wrong? And most importantly, why me? Is what I wanted to know.

That night, I consumed every drink that Wallace gave me.

"Make it a bit stronger," I told Wallace as I sat on the couch and handed the red plastic cup back to him.

"You need to calm down," he informed me.

I gazed at him and frowned.

I felt the alcohol was becoming my best friend. It kept me calm and smooth. I just wished I would have gone to the darn movies and out for ice cream. I should have known I wasn't ready to be in public, and the public wasn't prepared to accept me.

I cursed at my family and the horrible burden they had put on me. Their roots and their reputation had ruined my life, and it would forever ruin my life. As soon as I told someone who wasn't familiar with my culture that I was Haitian, they would automatically assume horrible things and pre-judge me.

I was sick and tired of the bull crap.

When Wallace came back with my maybe 10th or 11th drink, I hurriedly drunk it up and grabbed him by the hand.

I was so nervous my palms were sweaty and itchy.

He took his index finger and brushed my wild loose strands of hair out of my face.

"Are you okay?"

Batting my eyes, I stared into his beautiful brown mesmerizing ones. "I'm okay," I lied.

Heck no, I wasn't okay! I felt like I was about to vomit everywhere and perhaps pass out. I had drunk way more than what my body bargained for. Already, I was starting to feel dizzy.

"Let's go somewhere quiet and talk," Wallace suggested.

I was in no condition to refuse him.

As we got into the quiet room, I gazed at my surroundings. "It's hotttt in here," I slurred, easing back on the bed.

I grabbed my hair and placed it into a sloppy bun that rested on top of my head. Before I knew it, I was out.

"What the hell are you doing?" I cried as I opened my eyes.

The pain shooting between my thighs was excruciating. Unbearable pain that I never wished to feel so soon.

"Stop, Wallace!" I cried as I desperately tried with all my will to push him off me.

My tiny frame was no match for his athletic body. He was a damn football player for Christ sake! It was a lose-lose situation.

I squeezed my legs tighter and screamed for help.

My cries and pleas fell on deaf ears. Either no one heard me crying for help, or no one cared.

"Why are you doing this to me?" I asked him.

He stared into my eyes and let out an evil laugh.

Tears flowed down my cheeks. I grabbed him by his hair and began clawing at his face.

That didn't stop him. "STOP! STOP! PLEASE STOP!" I cried as I clawed up his face.

Turning my head, I could see the light in the hallway begin to dim. Then I saw a pair of feet at the door.

Finally, my cries are answered, or so I thought.

The door flung open.

"What in the hell are you doing with that witch?" I heard a female scream.

Wallace jumped off me.

"Thank you!" I screamed at the female.

"It's not what you think or what it looks like!" Wallace said in his defense.

I jumped up from the bed.

"And what do you mean by that?" she said with her hands balled into fists. I could see the tears gathering in her eyes.

Before the situation got uglier than it already was, I tried to make a run for it.

She stopped me at the door with the force of her body and sent one powerful kick to my stomach. It knocked me on my back. Within seconds, the room and the hallway were filled with onlookers.

"Beat that witch down, Thelma!" I heard people chanting as if seeing me getting beat up was their glory and their joy. I had done nothing to any of those people. What they thought of my family was their prerogative. It was evident that someone had put the hex on me, and I would forever be tortured.

Thelma did exactly what they cheered her on to do. She got on top of me and began punching me in my face, chest and anywhere else her powerful hands could reach.

"Please stop," I begged.

Finally, I began to fight her back. I grabbed a handful of her hair and she screamed bloody murder. I sent one kick to her stomach and made a run for it. My feet left fearful imprints in the red dirt as I ran back to my auntie's house.

"Abella! Why are you naked?" Adele screamed as she jumped up from her seat on the porch and ran to my aid.

I didn't even realize that I was naked. Staring down at my body, I noticed that I was wearing nothing more than my birthday suit. My body trembled with fear as pain shot from between my thighs and blood trickled down my legs.

Adele took off her long top, covered me up, and took me into the house and to her room. She went into her bathroom and ran bath water for me.

"Let's get you in the tub," Adele said.

She was my little cousin by three years, and she was now helping me as if she was the older one out of the two of us.

As soon as the hot water hit my precious jewels, I felt a bit of relief, but still broken and torn from what happened. Forget being humiliated. I was beyond humiliated.

Adele grabbed a wide toothbrush and began to brush my hair. As she patiently waited for me to talk to her, she opened her vocals.

"I see the bad moon arising ...

I see the trouble on the way ...

I see the earthquake and lighting ...

I see bad times today ... Born on the bayou... Born on the bayou... Born on the bayou ...." Adele had begun singing her own remix.

Her voice was the sweetest one could ever hope to hear. I always told her that she was going to be a famous singer one day, which was her dream as well. Her soothing vocals eased my mind and opened my heart.

I pushed my knees up to my chest as she continued to brush my hair.

"I just don't understand why don't anyone like us? What did we do wrong?" I questioned. The same question that I had asked myself day after day, but for years now, I had been unable to get a justifiable answer.

"We are not here for anyone to like us. People liking us doesn't serve any purpose at all. We got each other, and that's all that matters."

"Wallace raped me tonight," I stated, resting my head on my knees. *As I closed my eyes, the memory of what happened came back to my mind. I was never going to be able to forget what happened to me. I would be stuck with this horror for a lifetime.* *"Then Thelma jumped on me. Everyone stood around, laughed at me, and cheered her on. I hate Wallace and Thelma! I wish the both of them would just die."*

"They did what?" Adele asked in a soft yet angry tone.

I opened my hands and there rested a big chunk of Thelma's pretty little locks.

Adele grabbed the locks from my hands. *"Everything is going to be just fine,"* she assured me as she stuffed the locks into her pocket.

Later that night, I couldn't sleep. I tossed and turned all night long. Hearing the melody of Adele and my auntie singing, I eased out of the bed and tiptoed down the hallway.

Inside Adele's room, I saw them dancing around in a circle. The room was dark, and the only lights were from the candles. My aunt a weird tune as they danced around.

I stared down at Adele's hands and saw not one, but two little black dolls. My eyes zoomed in on the locks of Thelma's hair that I had given to Adele earlier. They were now on the doll's head.

The rumor about my family ritual was definitely the truth.

My aunt, Adias, was dressed in a black gown with her face painted. Some people associated the face paint with witch doctor paint. My aunt was very special; I had heard so many rumors about her healing and killing it was ridiculous.

Adele saw me peeping and frowned before she closed the door in my face.

I went back to my room and my head fell into my pillow as I cried myself to sleep.

I didn't go back to school for two weeks and three days to be exact. When I finally got back to school, all types of rumors had been spread about me. People couldn't wait until the day I arrived to torture my soul. I hadn't been in my first class for five minutes before students started to throw all sorts of verbal assaults at me. Then, when they saw the assaults weren't bothering me much, they started throwing paper and pencils at me. That's when I ran to the bathroom, and Summer found me.

Summer and I stood at the classroom door hand in hand, like little schoolgirls.

"Let's face the music together," she said as she let go of my hand and opened the classroom door.

As soon as we stepped inside the class, people started to make fun of us and throw things at us.

The teacher didn't once stop them.

I searched the room for Wallace and noticed that he wasn't sitting in his normal seat.

Summer's eyes scanned the room. I could look at her and tell that she was very upset. All the verbal assaults were taking a toll on her.

"LEAVE US ALONE! LEAVE US ALONE!" She screamed with her fists balled up.

"LEAVE US ALONE! LEAVE US ALONE!" I screamed along with her.

Summer began to turn a strange color. Hearing the lightning, I looked toward the windows and saw that it was getting dark outside. Lightning bolted from the sky and struck a tree. The oversized old tree leaned to its side. Lightning struck again, breaking three classroom windows. The class immediately hushed.

I grabbed Summer and wrapped my arms around her. Her body felt hot as hell.

"Please stop," I whispered in her ear as I kept my arms tightly wrapped around her.

I was no fool. I knew it was Summer who was causing all of the chaos.

Seconds later, all the chaos stopped.

I grabbed Summer by her hand and the two of us walked toward our assigned seats.

"You WITCHES GET THE HELL OUT OF MY CLASS!" Mrs. Maple yelled.

Mrs. Maple was dirt old. She had been around long enough to know about my family and what they were about. For that reason alone, she hated the sight of me.

She was always upsetting me. I heard her whispers amongst other teachers as she talked bad about my family when I walked down the hall. She thought I couldn't hear, but I was always able to hear her. As my aunt told me, I had a special gift and a part of that special gift was my ear.

Summer and I took our seats. The entire classroom got up and rushed to the door.

Mrs. Maple came from behind her desk and parted her lips to say something.

"Teach us!" Summer stood up and said with her arms crossed.

And that, Mrs. Maple did. She taught the two of us and the ringing of the bell dismissed class.

By the time we had gym, all sorts of rumors had circulated around the school. With Summer on my side and me on her side, we ignored all the rumors.

Later that day, I found out that Wallace's family had him transferred to another school. Good for him. He could run, but he sure as heck couldn't hide.

On my way to gym, Thelma brushed past me and rudely knocked me into a locker.

"Witch!" She said through gritted teeth as she stared me down.

"Don't pay her a mind," Adele said, walking up.

I followed Adele as she walked into the school's gym.

"Are you taking gym today?" Adele questioned.

"Do I ever?" I smiled.

She handed her bag to me while everyone got dressed for gym. I made my way outside and sat on the bleachers.

I hated gym, and I refused to run around in the hot sun getting all sweaty and messy. So, as always, I sat on the bleachers and watched the others participate.

As the class was running track, I sat holding Adele's bag in my arms.

Being nosey, I decided to peep and see what was in her bag that she always had me hold versus putting it in the lockers.

I opened the bag and peeped inside. I saw the same two dolls that Adele had the night before. One dolled favored Thelma, and the other was still plain.

Both dolls had pins in them. I was very familiar with the voodoo dolls as far as their looks, but that was just about it. This sort of stuff my family kept me away from.

I took a pin out of the doll that favored Thelma and stuck the pin back into the dolls stomach. I gazed at Thelma who was out on the field stretching. Nothing happened to her. I did it again and again, and still nothing happened.

I gazed at the doll and noticed a black string was hanging from the doll's neck. I grabbed both of the dolls and shoved them back in the book bag.

"What are you doing?" Summer asked, running toward me.

I tried to zip the bag up, but the string got caught in the zipper.

"Nothing." I smiled at Summer.

She grabbed Adele's book bag from me and tossed it on the bleacher.

"Let's race," she suggested.

"Not right now," I told her.

From behind her, I could see Thelma walking back inside.

Summer playfully bumped into me.

I sat down and she came behind me. "Let me do your hair in a French braid then," she said.

Before I could even answer, she took my ponytail out and began playing in my hair.

"AHHHH OH MY!" I heard someone scream.

The two of us, along with everyone on the field, stopped what we were doing and ran inside.

Hanging from the doorframe was Thelma's lifeless body. On the floor lay a brown wooden chair. The scene was horrifying. Although I couldn't stand her, I never wished death upon her. Tears began to run down my face. I quickly wiped them away.

"Give me my bag!" Adele said to me. She walked over and snatched her bag out of my hand.

"Don't play with fire or you'll get burned! The thoughts hurt way more and can do way more harm than death could ever do," she said softly through gritted teeth.

From that day on, Summer, Adele and I became a tight unit. The three of us were thick as thieves, a united front against an ignorant and intolerant community.

Chapter 2

Abella

Although Summer and I were busy with school throughout most of the year, every break, we would work in a local restaurant called Coco Hut. It was always packed, so we made excellent money, and the tips were the best! I was more skilled in Caribbean dishes, which is what Coco Hut specialized in, but Summer was awesome with her Creole recipes. She would even bring in crawfish that she caught herself. As time went on, and we showed our dedication by bringing in loyal customers, the owner started letting us spice the menu with our own creations.

Kreyol and Creole are two completely different backgrounds, but the one thing we had in common was the gift of magic and delicious food.

"Bonswa!" the owner would say every morning, which meant hello in Haitian Kreyol. She was a frail dark skinned woman with a head full of grey hair. She always wore colorful tribal scarves around her locks, which were accented with island seashells, and she always had a necklace made out of shark teeth around her neck.

Before she would open up shop, she would sage the whole spot and repeat it during closing time for good luck. When she talked, it was so fast and loud that if I weren't from the islands, I wouldn't understand a thing she was saying. I loved cooking, and I'm sure that's what birthed my habit of making dinner for my man was birthed.

Chapter 3

Summer

Miss Adias was like a mother to me. She taught me so much in my life. Most importantly, she was the one who taught me how to be a woman and how to love myself. I didn't have any momma figures in my life until I met her. My papa raised me the best he could, but he sure as heck didn't know anything about being a woman. From day one, she treated me as if I was her very own.

She was well known for being a 'thee' witch doctor around town. She was one of the best; she could heal or kill, or whatever it was. What you asked for is exactly what she gave you. As long as the price was right. She was about her money. The more money she made, the better life we lived.

After my father died, she took me into her home, and we became a tight little family. It was a relief to be surrounded by people who understood me, who possessed the same gift that I had often considered a curse. My heart shattered into millions of pieces the night she left us.

Abella, Adele and I were all in the house hanging out and talking about boys. We had just put Miss Adias' 'magical book' up. Had we been caught with it, she would have whipped us like it was no tomorrow, and then later severely punished us.

She had burst in the store, breathing heavily, with a wild look in her eyes. She ran around the room, closing all the shades and murmuring to herself.

"What's wrong, Momma?" Adele said.

Tears rolled down Ms. Adias' cheeks as she turned around to face us. I had never seen her cry, so it had to be something serious.

She rushed over to Adele, grabbed her and wrapped her arms around her. "Adele, look here," she said, holding her face, "I want you to know that no matter what, Momma loves you. I love you with all my heart. Girl, do you hear me?"

Adele shook her head as tears formed in her eyes. "Momma, what's going on?"

Miss Aidas went into the sack that she was carrying and pulled out a big wad of money. "Sometimes you get tired of fighting something you just can't fight no more. My purpose is you, and for you, I'll do anything," she said and wiped the tears from her face with the back of her hand.

"Momma, stop beating around the bush. What the hell is going on?"

Adele's arms hung to her side as she waited for her momma to give her an answer.

I glanced over at Abella, who was looking at me in confusion.

Miss Aidas wiped her face as she held her index finger under her nose. "Trouble has found me. I have to go, baby."

Adele knew what type of things her momma was into. She knew this day would eventually come. "Momma, no," Adele cried.

Abella and I rushed over to Adele and Miss Aidas and wrapped our arms around her.

She kissed us all on the forehead and rushed out the front door. We watched as she got into a black car and the car disappeared down the street. Heartbroken, Adele dropped to the floor and began to cry like a newborn baby. Her cries filled the house until she fell asleep.

My heart ached too. I had a different way of showing my feelings, and I always kept them in and hid them well. Deep down inside I was hurting; I wanted the momma I never had back. I wanted the maternal love I never had. That empty space that she filled was empty yet again. That was the last time we saw or even heard from Miss Aidas, the mother that I never had.

Things were rough for us after Ms. Adias left, but we stuck together and took care of each other. Adele was never the same after Ms. Adias left. She became reckless and partied all the time. Instead of going to college, as Abella and I had, she chose to work.

Abella tried her best to fill Ms. Adias shoes, but she was no substitute for a mother. We both just did the best we could to keep Adele out of trouble.

Chapter 4

Abella

I sipped on my drink as I watched my girls mingle with random guys. I only drank dark now, Southern Comfort or Jack Daniels. There are way too many evil stories featuring vodka and moonshine in my memory bank. Vodka is the devil's juice, or so I'd been told. It was Mardi Gras weekend, and it seemed that everybody and their momma was in my neck of the woods. I grabbed my colorful mask. It was accented with glitter and rhinestones that resembled an old French queen's jewelry, and feathers so big it looked like a tribe of Choctaw Indians had put them on there.

I put the mask over my face, barely covering it. Easing through the crowd, I made my way to the middle of the dance floor. With my head back, I began to swing my hips to the loud music. Partiers were drunk and hyped, and no one was on beat! Reminded me of an old Cajun hoedown from my childhood.

Summer tapped me on my shoulder. "Hey, Abella!"

I turned around, grabbed her, and together the two of us danced wildly to the loud music. I was happy that we all were able to get out and enjoy ourselves. We didn't get much 'us' time as we would have liked.

"Where's Adele?" I questioned Summer as we walked out of the club.

She shrugged. "I don't know, she was talking to that boy with the dreads earlier."

I stared hard at Summer. She was lying, I could tell. I snatched the mask off my face. "Where the hell is she?" I yelled as I grabbed Summer by her shoulders.

I could feel the anger growing inside me. Over the years, I'd learned that my gift could do me or others harm if I didn't control it. Me getting angry didn't do my special gift any good. I bit my bottom lip and stared at Summer for an answer.

"She left with that boy," Summer said and lowered her eyes.

"She left with that boy?" I mocked. "That boy with all those friends with him?"

I shook my head and sat on the curb to calm myself down before I got too angry. I was pissed at myself for allowing my cousin to get out of my sight. It was like I turned my head for one damn second, and just like that, she had disappeared. It didn't hurt to say that I was my cousin's keeper, and she was my keeper. We were all we had, and we made a vow years ago to have each others back at all times.

Summer came and sat beside me. "I tried to call her several times, but I didn't get an answer."

I turned around and stared into Summer's beautiful innocent eyes. I could see that she was telling the truth. She honestly didn't know where Adele had run off to.

"Je t'aime." Summer smiled.

"I love you more," I replied as I stared off into the street.

"Let's just go home and wait for her to come home or to call us. I'm sure she's okay," Summer said.

I shook my head, agreeing with her. We waved a taxi down and went back to our home.

———————

The next morning, I woke up bright and early with a mean headache. I had only gotten about two hours of sleep tops. My little cousin, Adele, was on my mind all night long. I picked up the phone and tried her cell phone. It went to voicemail. I kept calling, in hopes of getting a response.

I swallowed the lump in my throat as I thought about who to call next. I then remembered, Aida, my aunt Adias' evil twin sister, whom Adele had been talking to a lot lately.

They were closer when they were younger, but as we got older, they grew apart. Aida and Adias were very different from each other. Adias was the laid-back one. You don't mess with her she won't mess with you. But she also had very vindictive ways. She could be worse than any karma. She would come for you when you least expected. Nothing got past her. But, she was never the one who went looking for trouble. Now, my aunt, Aida, on the other hand, that woman was a firecracker. She could be your worst nightmare. She was very vindictive and evil for no reason. I felt as if she was born with no heart; she had no cares in the world.

Despite her being mean and evil, my aunt Aida was a gorgeous woman. She was tall with a lovely slim body. Men knew about her, yet they ignored all the horrid rumors that the town spread and tried to shack up with her. Aida just had that effect on folks, with her angelic looks. She had long greyish hair that hung to the middle of her back. Her hair was a natural grey. My aunt, Adias told me that her hair had been like that ever since she was a young girl. She would say that it came that way from all the stress she endured as she grew up. Regardless of how she adopted the greyish colored hair, it looked beautiful on her, and she wore it with nothing but pride. Her skin was a tad darker than mine; it was sort of like a milky way brown with no flaws whatsoever.

Her eyes were a midnight blue with a slight hint of grey. Very enticing and magical. It seemed that if her eyes were stared upon too hard, you would forever be locked in her magical world, where only her rules existed and none other. My Aunt had been married twelve times that we know of. All of her husbands had some sort of unsolved mystery behind them. Kids, she didn't have any of her own. She was once pregnant. That was the most joyful I had ever seen her. When she was pregnant, she glowed every second of the day. Sometimes, we would actually catch her with a small smile. She came around every day, showcasing her protruding little belly. Then one day, she just stopped coming around.

Later, we found out that she had lost her son. After giving birth to her stillborn son and nearly losing her mind as she blamed and cursed half the town for his death, she settled on not having any kids. She just couldn't bear the hurt again. Since that day, she's lived her life isolated from the world.

"Aunt Aida," I cooed in a soft voice as soon as I heard her pick up the phone.

She didn't say a word, but her breathing signaled that she was still on the line. For confirmation, I glanced down at my cell, which read nineteen seconds talk time.

"Aida, I know you are on the phone. Say something." I sighed. She was so damn weird that it made no sense.

"It's me, Abella." I huffed.

"What do you want? And who sent you, Abella?" Aida asked.

I hated that this woman was so darn paranoid. Life had taken a toll on her.

"Aida, no one sent me——" I said before she rudely cut me off.

"Adele is not here. I haven't spoken to her. News will come soon," she replied and hung the phone up in my ear.

"You weirdo!" I hypocritically said to myself and dialed her number back. This time her phone was off.

I eased out of bed and went into the bathroom to shower, brush my teeth and get my day started.

After I got dressed, I sat on the couch and called every jail and hospital in New Orleans, and still there was no word on Adele. My gut feeling told me the worst, yet I still tried to remain positive.

Chapter 5

Summer

My stomach did cartwheels as I walked into the house and noticed Abella sitting on the couch with sadness painted all over her cherubic face. I hated to see my best friend looking all down and depressed.

"What's up?" I asked as I eased onto the couch next to her.

She turned to face me and shrugged. "I don't know. I haven't heard from her yet."

Tears rolled down her cheeks. My eyes started to burn as well. I couldn't stop the tears.

I jumped up from the couch and rushed into the kitchen. My hand shook as I grabbed us two cold pops. Before going back into the living room, I needed to get myself together. I turned the kitchen sink on to tune out any noise, and banged my fist against the kitchen counter.

I had been up all night thinking about Adele, and on top of that, I got up early to search the streets. No one had seen her nor heard from her.

In the pit of my stomach, I had an ominous feeling that something bad had happened to Adele. That feeling had never once failed me. It was always right. With the back of my hands, I wiped the tears from my face, grabbed our pops, and headed back into the living room.

"Everything is going to be okay. We will find her today." I made a promise to my friend as I handed her the pop.

I grabbed the remote controller off the table and began flicking through the television channels. Glancing over at Abella, I noticed she hadn't touched her pop, and she still had that sad look on her face.

I knew Adele meant a lot to her. They were best friends and cousins. True blood ...

"Hey, lets go check Sunny's house out. Maybe she and Adele started back talking," I suggested to Abella.

A smile crept across her face as she joyfully jumped from the couch and ran to retrieve her slide ons.

Sunny and Adele used to be best friends. Those two were like bees to honey. When you saw one, you would see the other, but a small incident had happened between the two, and since then, they had kind of fell apart.

One day, Sunny, Abella, Adele and I had all decided to be grown and sneak to a boy's house. Adele had a big crush on this guy, so we decided to just go hang out. After sitting on their porch all day, we had so much fun that we didn't realize time had passed by so quickly.

"I have to hurry up and get home. It's dark outside," Sunny whined.

We all knew how her parents were, and none of us were trying to hear their mouths.

"Let's just take the short cut," Adele suggested, not wanting her best friend to get in any trouble on her behalf.

We said our goodbyes to the boys and began to walk down the long dark street. None of us feared a thing, or should I say Abella, Adele and I didn't fear a thing. If anything, folks feared us. As we were walking, I noticed Adele holding Sunny's hand tightly. I snickered to myself and shook my head.

We reached the graveyard and Sunny was damn near in tears. She was even shaking a bit.

"Grow up, you big cry baby," I hissed.

I wasn't trying to be mean, but that girl was always crying over the littlest things. She really needed to grow herself a set of steel balls.

She glared at me and rolled her eyes.

Adele snatched her hand as the two of them began to walk fast in front of us.

"Adele and Sunny, sitting in the tree. K-I-S-S-I-N-G." I cracked myself up as I teased the two. One would have thought the two of them were girlfriends, as close as they were.

Abella began to laugh a bit, then playfully shoved me. Signaling for me to cut out the teasing.

I lightly tapped Abella on her arm. She stared at me and we both burst into laughter. The two of us together were silly.

"You know it's the truth. This graveyard is really haunted," I yelled out, trying to scare Sunny.

"Don't walk away from us. If the ghosts come out, Adele won't be able to save you by herself," Abella added.

The two of us laughed some more.

"Nous en venons à réveiller tous de vous. Pour libérer vos âmes. Vivre parmi nous. Respirer avec nous. Vous êtes libre. Libre je dit! Vous êtes libre!" I yelled out.

"Wake up! You are FREE! FREE to live, free to breathe. We are freeing you," Abella added.

"Réveiller l'enfer! Je vous gratuitement. Vous libérant maintenant."

Sunny turned back around. "What are y'all doing? Y'all stop that now!"

Adele stopped in her tracks and turned around to face us. "Stop—" She began. Her eyes grew big as a loud noise filled our ears. Loud noises that I'd never heard before nor cared to ever hear again.

"What the hell?" Adele screamed.

I turned around, following her eyes, and noticed a big black shadow. The noise began to get louder.

None of us said a word. Adele took off running.

Sunny turned around, tried to run, and fell flat on her face.

"My ankle. My ankle." She screamed in agony.

I was scared, and I couldn't care less about her ankle. I jumped right over her pleasantly plum tail and kept it moving.

When I looked behind me, it seemed the shadow was getting closer by the second.

Abella, feeling guilty, helped Sunny to her feet. Sunny used her as a crutch and the two of them picked up pace.

Needless to say, Adele was the first person home.

We ran in the house behind her, and found her standing in her dark bedroom, screaming some weird things.

The sound grew louder and louder. Sunny glanced out the window and instantly fainted. Whatever she saw had knocked her right off her feet.

The sound was loud and unbearable; it felt like the windows to the house were about to shatter.

"What the hell is going on in here?" Adele's mother screamed as she entered the room and turned the lights on. The sound we were hearing instantly went away.

"We are just playing," Adele barely managed to say.

Her mother threw her hands on her hips. "Y'all better be just playing," she said before walking out the room.

Later, Sunny started to act weird and said that strange things were going on at her house. After that, none of us ever spoke about what happened, and Sunny never mentioned what she saw that night.

Sunny's parents were super religious and were stuck on the idea that Adele had brought some kind of bad spirit into their home. From that day forward, they wouldn't allow Sunny to hang out with Adele. At times, the two of them would sneak and hang out. Every time Sunny was caught going against her parent's rules, she was always punished. After a while, she got tired of being punished and stopped hanging out with Adele.

Abella and I laughed at the memory as we walked down the long red dirt road. When we arrived at the entrance to the graveyard, we stopped in our tracks and looked at each other. We hadn't been back to or through that graveyard since the stuff happened with Sunny.

It was as if Abella and I were reading each other's mind as we stood at the entrance.

"I ain't scared of nothing," Abella stated with a shrug of her shoulders and walked into the graveyard.

"Me either," I stated and walked behind her.

On our way to Sunny's house, we didn't say a word.

Sunny's house was directly on the bayou. We took our shoes off and called her name while standing out front.

I put my hand up to my face to block the sun.

"Sunny, we know you are in there, just come out for a second," I yelled up at a window.

The curtain moved from side to side. I could see Sunny's face hiding within the sheerness of the curtain.

"If you can see us, better believe we can see you." I laughed.

"What do y'all want?" Sunny yelled out the window.

Rumors were going around that Sunny was some sort of weirdo. It didn't dawn on me until that moment that Sunny was super paranoid. I hope that whatever she saw that night hadn't scared her to where she lived a life filled with fear.

"Have you seen or heard from Adele?" Abella asked.

Sunny scrunched her nose up and closed the curtain. In a matter of seconds, she was opening the front door.

She looked a mess, wearing a long black sheer dress filled with holes. Her disheveled hair was all over the place.

"No, I haven't seen nor heard from her. What is going on?" Sunny asked worriedly.

"She's been missing for a day or so, and I'm just getting a bit worried," Abella answered.

"A bit worried? Are you sure everything is okay?" Sunny asked again. The look on her face told that she still had love for Adele.

"I'm sure everything is just fine," I said.

"When you find her, let me know. Please come back and give me word," Sunny said.

Abella shook her head in agreement. "Have a nice day."

I waved back to Sunny with a smirk.

We walked back through the graveyard. Soon as we got close to the house, Abella went crazy, knocking on everyone and anybody's door, trying to find Adele.

"Calm down, Abella." I gripped her up by her arm.

"Find her now!" She screamed and yanked her arm away from me.

Our eyes locked for a split second. She then turned around and began walking to the house. I felt helpless and hopeless. There was nothing that I could do but just continue to look for my friend.

When we got the house, Abella ran up to her room. I could hear her bedroom door slam. A few minutes later, some unfamiliar sounds. I ran upstairs just in time to catch Abella destroying her room. Every time she got upset, she let loose and began to destroy things. She had no control whatsoever.

"Ahhh!" She screamed as she threw a frame against the wall. The picture hit the wall and shattered into pieces.

Looking around her room, I noticed the bed was flipped over, clothes everywhere, along with other broken things. Abella was red and hot; she was ready to lose it.

I had to duck before she accidentally took my head off when she threw another picture toward the door. I reached down and grabbed the photograph; it was a photo of Adele, Abella and me that Miss Adias had taken.

Abella threw herself on the floor and began to have a big hissy fit like a small child.

I turned the picture over and the back of it read, 'My favorite three.'

I walked over to Abella and dropped to the floor next to her. "Everything is going to be okay," I told her.

She scooted closer to me and laid her head in my lap. I began to play in her curls.

"Abella," I spoke in a calm voice, "Let's go out there and find Adele. We won't come back until we find her."

Her watery filled eyes stared into mine. "Okay," she said and got up from the floor to get herself together.

We hit the streets again, carrying Adele's picture in our hands. Abella was a few feet in front of me. She was about to knock on another door until her cell phone rang. She snatched it out of her jean shorts pocket.

"Hello," Abella panted.

I stared at her as I tried to hear her conversation.

"It's Adele!" Abella said.

She took off running and I ran right behind her.

As we ran in the direction of the hospital, my heart dropped. My gut feeling was telling me that this wasn't good at all.

We made it to the hospital in ten minutes, tops. Abella, sweaty and out of breath, rushed through the emergency room entrance. Passing by the help desk, she hurried through the hospital like a mad woman.

"Adele! Adele!" She screamed as she frantically ran through the halls.

She was moving so fast she started to give me a headache. I ran the other way as she continued to scream Adele's name and rip curtains from random folks' room.

My heart dropped as I entered my second room. Although she wasn't recognizable, I knew it was her. I had felt her presence standing in front of her door.

"Adele. Oh my, Adele," I cried.

I couldn't believe what I saw as I eased into the room, which was filled with beeps from several life support machines. I rushed over to Adele's side and grabbed her swollen hand. She was in bad shape. Her face was bandaged. Her lips were busted, it was horrible.

I could feel my temper rising.

"Adele." I began to panic. My chest heaved up and down. I was seconds away from overheating. Desperately, I tried to shake the devastating feeling, but I just couldn't.

My hands began to shake uncontrollably. Biting down on my bottom lip, I tried yet again to shake the desperate urge that was breaking through me like a wild beast.

I was HURT, ANGRY, UPSET!

Who in their right mind would do this to Adele? Who? No one treats a human being like this!

The curtains began to sway back and forward. The window that was behind me flung open.

"WHO DID THIS?" I said to Adele as if she could speak.

Hell hath no fury like a woman who was PISSED off!

"Summer!" I heard Abella's voice behind me.

The window swung shut and the curtains instantly stopped swaying.

Abella took a deep swallow, then slowly walked to Adele's bedside.

"Adele..." she whispered as tears slowly fell down her cheeks.

Chapter 6

Abella

Lost for words, I stood next to Adele's bed and stared at her. She appeared to be in so much pain. At that second, I wished I had powers to heal, so I could just erase all her pain with just a touch.

I had to find someone to heal my cousin. There were folks out there who could heal her, I just had to find someone. I touched her face, gently running my hands down her swollen cheeks. I took the strands of hair that were in her face and pushed them back. One thing Adele didn't like was loose strands of hair all in her face. Her skin was so damn pale. I had never in my life seen Adele looking bad like this.

My mind was all over the place.

"Get me a brush and some makeup. She looks horrible. Just look at her." I began to cry.

I turned around to Summer, who was staring out the window.

"I can't have Adele looking like this, Summer."

Summer shook her head in agreement.

My heart ached, seeing my cousin lying there fighting for her life. Who in the hell did this to her? We bothered no one! We stayed to ourselves. What did we do to deserve this? All sorts of questions raced through my mind.

"Are you going to be okay by yourself while I go to the house and get some of Adele's things?" Summer asked.

Not once taking my eyes off Adele, I shook my head yes.

When I felt Summer's presence leave the room, I grabbed Adele's face and opened her eyelids. A while back, I had discovered something that Adele told me was dangerous and I should leave it alone.

I was at the store buying groceries and other stuff we needed for the house. A guy kept following me down the aisle. "May I help you?" I asked him to see what exactly he wanted. The first thing I noticed about him was his pleasant smile; the second was his sandy brown hair. Finally, I acknowledged how handsome he was.

"You are just so beautiful, I just couldn't help but introduce myself," he stated with the most gorgeous smile I'd ever seen. He extended his right had. "I'm Steven."

"I'm Abella." I shook his hand and held on t for a second longer than I had anticipated, seeing things I didn't want to see. Things I shouldn't have seen. I quickly let his hand go. "Well, Steven, I shall see you around." I quickly dismissed myself.

After I had discovered one of my gifts, I called Adele in my room to test it on her.

"Abella, we are a different kind of person. We are not like the rest. Whoever created us spent extra time creating us." Adele had advised me as she grabbed both of my hands.

I squeezed Adele's hands tightly and closed my eyes.

Adele snatched her hands from me. Again, I grabbed her hands, pressing my palms into hers with my eyes closed.

My eyes flew open when a harsh slap assaulted my face.

"Abella, stop it! You can't just go around town reading folks' minds and thoughts!"

"Are you hiding something?"

"No! Leave what you discovered alone. It's very dangerous. You will get back what you dish out. I want to leave all of this in the past. Let the special gifts be! I want to be normal for once!" She walked to my bedroom door. "Abella, leave it alone," she had warned me once more before leaving the room.

My hands slowly eased to Adele's hands. Her words were stuck in my head, yet I was desperate to know who had done this and why.

I traced over Adele's swollen hands with the tip of my index finger. Pausing, I gave a quick thought to what I was about to do. I had to know. There was no way that anyone was going to get away with hurting my little cousin.

Closing my eyes, I squeezed her palm tightly.

I could see Adele standing in front of the bar, speaking to a very handsome guy. He was saying all sorts of sweet things to Adele, had her wide open. She blushed as she burst into laughter.

I jumped as I heard a knock. Two police officers walked in.

"Hello there," one of them said.

"May I help you?" I said with an attitude.

I knew they were there to help, but I couldn't care less. I didn't need their help. This situation was close to being handled.

"You must be Abella?"

I shook my head yes. "Whatever you are here for, we are just fine."

"Okay, that's not how this works. We have a few questions," the tall, slim Caucasian officer said as he whipped out a notepad.

"Questions for who? I don't know anything."

The chubby black officer decided to take control of the situation. "Look, miss, we are here to help you, and that's it. Your cousin has been raped, beaten and is now fighting for her life. We have a few questions to ask, and after that, we will leave you alone. We are just here to do our job."

The mention of rape was a painful jab to the chest. I had been in that same boat before, and it was nothing easy to deal with or get over.

My mind went back to the time when I was raped. I could feel the pain as if it was happening that second. A rush of pure hatred flooded my heart.

"So you guys were hanging out at a local bar?" the officer asked, bringing me back to the present.

"Yes," I replied.

"Do you remember who she was talking to? Did you see her leave with anyone?"

I shook my head no. "I was drunk. I don't recall anything about that night."

"You don't recall anything?" he asked with the raise of his eyebrow.

"Nothing at all." I shook my head.

He glanced over at his partner then back at me. "Well, we are sorry to bother you, Miss. If you remember anything, you can contact either of us. Here," he said and handed over a piece of paper. "We hope your cousin gets well soon."

"Thank you," I replied and walked them to the door.

I watched as the two of them walked down the hall. Back at the bed, I grabbed Adele's hands.

"You are going to show me what happened."

Chapter 7

Abella

Tears ran down my cheeks as I yanked my hands away.

"Why you? Why did he have to do this to you?" I cried as I questioned my cousin, who wasn't able to give me an answer.

I ran my hands down her warm face and planted a kiss on her cheek. "He won't get away with this."

The horrid sight I just had seen had my mind everywhere. Standing in the door frame, I gazed back at my cousin with a face full of hurt, tears rolling down my face.

I turned around and raced toward the hospital exit.

"Abella!" Summer said as I nearly knocked her onto the floor.

She grabbed me by my shoulders. "Is everything okay?"

"I just can't see her like that," I stated, not mentioning that I knew way more than I should know, more than I had anticipated knowing.

"Okay, go home, and I'll stay here. I'll see you soon," she said.

I shook my head as fresh tears gathered in my eyes.

"I love you," Summer said and wrapped her arms around me.

The scent of her perfume tickled my nostrils. I pulled myself back from her grip, stared into her eyes. "I love you too."

I watched as she turned and disappeared down the hallway.

When I stepped outside, it was a bit dark. I thought about which way to walk home and decided to walk through the graveyard.

I wasn't afraid of a thing. If anything was in that graveyard, it had better be afraid of me tonight. The way I was feeling, I could destroy anything or anyone. Just as I made it to the corner from the hospital, the rain started, and then the thunder and lightening followed. I walked down the street in a world of my own, ignoring the horns honking and the rides that were offered to me.

Standing at the entrance to the graveyard, I took a deep breath. I feared nothing as I moved amongst the stones.

"Réveillez l'enfer! Ressuscitez d'entre les morts! Je dois ici vous libérer! Je dois ici vous libérer maintenant! (Wake the hell up! Rise from the dead! I'm here to free you! I'm here to free you now!')" I screamed at the top of my lungs.

The thunder grew louder as it rained harder. I raised my hands to the sky as I felt something different, something I'd never felt before running through my body. It was magical, sort of like an electric shock.

Lightning struck and hit a tombstone in front of me.

I dropped to my knees; a wicked laugh escaped my mouth as tears ran down my face. As I jumped to my feet and began dancing in the rain, the loud horrifying noise that I had heard years ago when Adele, Sunny, Summer and I had run through the graveyard filled the air. I then saw the big black thing running toward me.

I did not move. I wasn't afraid at all. "I'm not scared," I said with a smirk as I jumped forward with my hand raised in the air.

I burst into laughter as I realized that not only can I be someone else's worst nightmare, I was my own worst nightmare.

"I'll be damn," I spoke aloud before bursting into laughter again.

The big black thing that had followed us that night was only following us because it belonged to one of us. It was mine! My shadow!

Chapter 8

Summer

I hated to see Adele hooked up to all those machines, fighting for her life. As I sat in the chair, staring at her hard as possible, my eyes felt as if they were burning a hole in her soul. I wished and wished that I had some sort of special power that I could use to wake her up. Bring her back to life and erase the horrible memories that would cause her pain, hatred, and misery.

Staring at the clock on the wall, I noticed that it was a little past visiting hours. I had already been told so three times, but I didn't pay them any mind. I would leave when I felt like doing so. The ongoing ticking and the sounds of the life support machine that Adele was connected to began to drive me crazy.

I got up from my chair and stared at Adele as she laid there lifeless. The machine caused her chest to heave up and down every few seconds.

Leaning over, I kissed her on her cheeks. "I love you, girl."

Before leaving the room, I glanced back at her one more time. With a face full of pain and a heavy heart, I held my head down and walked out the hospital.

I thought about walking home but I was way too drained to do so. Life was draining the hell out of me. Instead, I decided to take a taxi. The entire ride, I thought about a whole new life. I wanted to get far away from New Orleans and find a better me. When my papa died, I should have left and never come back.

Being here in New Orleans had created nothing but a monster...

When I pulled up to the house, I noticed it was pitch black dark, except for a ray of light coming from Abella's room. I softly closed the door and eased into the house.

I could hear loud music and Abella screaming over the top of the music as I approached her room. When I cracked the door open, I saw her rocking back and forth on the floor. The legs of a small doll hung from her lap. The room was filled with candles, in front of her lap rested an oversized book.

Shaking my head, I closed the bedroom door back. Abella was really losing it. If she loses Adele, I could only imagine how the entire world was going to feel her wrath.

I was just about to hop in the shower when I heard Abella's door slam shut. I rushed to my door and got a glimpse of her walking down the steps dressed in a black dress. She was humming a tune as she moved.

I made it to the window in time to see her walking in the middle of the street as if she was invisible. I didn't even question to see where she was going or what she was up to. After I showered, I laid in bed with a picture of my papa. Sad and depressed, I cried myself to sleep.

Chapter 9

Abella

Karma? Hmmm, karma had nothing on Abella. I was tired and fed up with my family and I being treated a certain way. We were humans and we deserved to be treated like humans. Everything about this guy, I could see it. I felt as if I could smell him. I had pure hatred burning in my soul.

I blinked, trying to stop the tears as I walked up to his house.

Adele's screams filled my ears. Her begging him no, screaming for him to please stop. My body shook uncontrollably as I felt her pain run through me.

Taking a deep breath, I rang the doorbell. After a few seconds, he came to the door dressed in a pair of boxers with black socks on his feet. He was really handsome. I could see why Adele fell for him.

Lifting my hands up, I blew the black dust in his face. His eyes watered immediately.

The man who had violated my cousin stepped his right foot outside the doorframe, no doubt looking for the gorgeous female who was just standing at his doorstep. He then stepped back in the house. Closed the door and opened it, as if I was going to magically appear again.

I stood right behind him, watching his everyone move. My beauty was always someone's downfall.

He closed the door and opened it again.

"Michael," I whispered.

As soon as my voice hit the air, it began to echo. Standing off to the side, I watched as he slammed the door closed and began to frantically search his living room.

Moments later, after finding nothing, he grabbed his head as if he was going crazy. Slowly, he walked up the stairs, with me tipping right behind him. He never noticed I was right on his heels, not once did he realize I was about to become a part of him.

Minutes later, he was back in his bed. "Michael," I whispered, removing my dress and climbing on top him.

His eyes flew open as my lips touched his and my bare body moved against his chest. He opened his mouth as if he was going to say something.

"Shhh," I told him, putting my hands up to his lips.

I threw my head back. My curls ran free like a wild stallion. I looked into his eyes and let out an evil laugh.

"What the hell!" he screamed and threw me off of him. My body hit the floor like a sac of potatoes.

Standing up, I stared at my image in the floor length mirror. Face covered in black and white, eyes of hurt and pain. A looked favored by the witch doctor when she was about to turn days into cold lonely and fearful nights.

Impressed with my skills, I let out a loud wicked laugh.

Michael grabbed his chest and turned to run down the stairs. He could run, but he sure as hell couldn't hide. He was going to feel Adele's pain, feel the pain that he'd caused me.

He fell backwards on his rear end at the bottom of the stairs when he noticed the candle lit living room.

"Michael," I whispered as I floated near him. "Michael."

His chest heaved up and down, as if he was nearing a heart attack.

I rushed over to him and removed his hand from his chest. "Don't be afraid," I told him in a sweet voice.

The frightened look of death was in his eyes. He rushed back upstairs.

"Michael, why are you running from me? Don't you want to play?" I yelled.

The thunder from outside roared like a raging lion. I could see the lightening through the curtains.

"MICHAEL!" I yelled as the windows and every door in the house began to open and slam shut.

"Where are you, Michael?" I spoke in a calm sweet voice as I searched for him.

From a room at the end of the hall, I heard a loud sound. I walked to the room and opened the door. Sadness fell over me as I saw his lifeless body on the ground, with a still smoking gun in his hand.

"Aww, I wanted to have some fun," I said as I stood at his stiff feet.

Chapter 10

Abella

It seemed that I had just gotten to sleep. My night consisted of tossing and turning, and the ongoing nightmare that invaded my slumber every night of my life. I sat on the edge of my bed and took a sip of my water. Getting up from the bed, I walked the house, something that I normally did.

"Summer?" I called out as I opened her door.

I could hear her snoring like a baby. She must have just gotten in from work or something. Being the friend she was, she was pulling extra weight as I got myself together.

I closed the door, went back to my room and got into bed. Finally, I was able to drift off into a peaceful sleep.

"ABELLA!" Summer screamed, scaring the life out of me.

"What?" I asked, taking a deep breath. The worried look on her face caused my heart to sink. "What is it?" I asked again.

"It's Adele. She's up."

I jumped out of bed and slid on a pair of shorts and a tank top. Without even lacing my shoes, I took off running to the hospital. Summer was right on my heels.

At the hospital, I rushed through the glass doors. Not wasting time on the elevator, I jogged the six flights of stairs up to her room, taking the steps two by two.

"Adele." My heart raced as I burst into her room.

She sat up in her bed. A smile crept across her face as she saw me.

I rushed over and hugged the life out of her. "I love you so much," I cried as tears escaped my eyes.

Summer ran over and wrapped her arms around us. The three of us hugged and cried and cried. Losing each other was one of our worst fears. The three of us were all we had, all we knew, and all we wanted to know. It was the three us, always and forever, against the world.

I sat in the chair next to the bed watching as Summer fixed Adele's hair for her. Gazing out the window, I began to execute a plan for my cousin, my best friend and myself. Things had to change. I had to find a better way for us.

In my stomach, I had a weird feeling that something terrible was about to happen. I couldn't put my finger on it because everything was going well. Ignoring the feeling, I stood up. My heart sank to the pit of my stomach as I saw the wicked witch from hell walking up to the hospital.

I turned around to say something to Adele, but my words stuck in my throat as she began to choke. Summer patted her back, as I rushed over to the nearby table and grabbed a glass of water and tried to give it to Adele. Her eyes filled with tears and her already pale skin grew even paler.

"Huhuhu …" Adele tried to say something. Her chest heaved up and down at a fast pace.

"DOCTOR! DOCTOR!" I ran into the hall and to the nurses station.

I ran back to the room and Adele was still trying to catch her breath. The frightened look in her eyes, I will never forget.

Everything was a blur; the room began to spin as it started to get really hot. Seconds later, I woke up to see doctors surrounding Adele's bedside. Summer stood in the doorframe. Her eyes were wide as saucers and her hand covered her mouth.

"ONE-TWO-THREE," I heard one of the doctors desperately scream as she tried to resuscitate Adele.

They tried and tried.

"NOOOO!" someone screamed.

Coming in the room from behind Summer was Aunt Aida, dressed in all black, with a black veil over her face.

"Vous! C'est vous qui avez tué ma nièce. Chaque depuis que vous êtes arrivée autour de l'arrière chance est tombé sur nous. Vous êtes maudits! Vous allez mourir dans la douleur et brûle en enfer!" She stared into my eyes.

Biting my lip, to force myself not say anything, I wondered how dare she come in his hospital and blame me for anything. She was the curse not me.

"You bitter heffa! You caused us to live in misery. You are the reason why half the town hates us. We are cursed because of you. Spreading your legs all across town, shacking up with women's men and then cursing them. You die, you miserable old witch!" I screamed back at her.

Seeing the family in such an uproar, the doctors excused themselves. Not wanting to get caught in the cross fire, Summer had a seat against the windowsill.

Aida walked over to Adele's body and began praying over her. She went in her purse and pulled out something, which she began to spread over Adele. After she took the black veil off, she rested it over top of Adele's lifeless face.

"You stop that now!" I cried, snatching the veil away from Adele's face, "Haven't you brought us enough heartache and pain?"

She stared deep into my eyes as if she was reading my soul. I waited for her to say something.

"It will all come back to you four times worse." She laughed as she walked out the room. "Four times worse," I heard her say again as she walked down the hall.

"Why, Adele? Why?" I cried.

Chapter 11

Summer

I could easily see the reflection of myself in my shoes as I looked down. Black, shiny, patent leather shoes that I couldn't wait to wear to a popping party on Bourbon. I couldn't wrap my mind around the fact that this is where I debuted them. Adele was gone. She would never be here in the physical anymore. Her soul had moved on to another dimension. I wondered if she still remembered us, wherever she was. All of us here … at her funeral.

I arrived early to ensure that her service was going to go smoothly. You know how it is. Funeral directors don't care. They just want their money. I mean, who even knows whose body is in the casket unless it is open. Or if the ashes in the urn aren't just from a candle that happened to burn out over night because someone forgot to blow it out. I can only imagine how many people have been buried alive. Well, this was an open casket funeral. It was definitely Adele resting in the white cushions of her new bed. The funeral home was still empty, and people wouldn't be arriving for another thirty minutes. I went to have another word with Adele's vacant body before everyone who loved her arrived.

As I looked down in her casket, I saw her forehead perspiring. It was so hot this Sunday. I felt bad for all the people who were trying to rest in the graveyard underneath the blazing sun, with no air conditioning.

As I looked at her, so many memories ran through my head. It's as if she was just a chapter in my life. I realized we wouldn't be making any new moments together. "Adele, I will always miss you. You are now my guardian angel. I know you will always have my back like you promised," I said.

I waited there like she was going to respond. Maybe she did and I didn't notice. It did seem as if the corners of her mouth changed. I assumed she was smiling.

The funeral directors started to gather at the door. I saw people arriving. Everyone but her family. Not that she had much family anyway. We were her family. Maybe they just couldn't handle what had happened. Her aunt isn't even here. But who am I to judge? The funeral directors were handing out obituaries to everyone who entered the glass double doors. Within minutes, the service was packed. Crowded with big sun hats, veils, and fans flapping back and forth, recycling the hot air inside the country chapel. The faint sounds of crying filled the room.

I sat in the back, trying to disappear under my big black hat that made me look like a black widow spider. *This outfit is ridiculous,* I thought to myself as I scratched at the lace from my stockings. Where is Abella? I quickly realized she wasn't there yet. She was closer to Adele than I was.

As if she read my mind, I heard her voice behind me.
"I'm here," she said as she sat down beside me.

Abella was wearing a colorful dress with feathers in
her hair. It was just like her to represent Haiti at a funeral.
Crazy ass. Well, I guess I am representing Louisiana
Creole. Looking like a witch and what not. I giggled. I
guess we could leave it up to Abella to bring a little life
to a day when we are celebrating death, because I was
wearing nothing but black.

"Do you think Sunny is going to come?" I asked
Abella.

She shrugged. I mean, things had never been the
same between them. But out of respect, I would think she
would at least come and say goodbye. Everyone in the
chapel was old; teachers, co-workers and other people
who had stayed after their church services. To be honest,
if they hadn't stayed, it would've been pretty empty.
Bless their souls. I didn't recognize hardly anyone. The
organ started playing. Oh my gosh. This has really
happened. My friend was gone, all because of a man who
put his hands on her and beat her into a coma.

I hoped Abella would be able to control her powers
during this service. I would hate for Adele's body to sit
up straight in the casket or for the chapel's stained glass
windows to start bursting.

I looked over at her. She was calm, twirling her hair
and chewing on her nails. No one went up and spoke on
Adele's behalf. I didn't because I felt somewhat
responsible for what had happened to her. I stopped
Abella from going up there. Nothing good was going to
come out of that. Speaking in tongues right now is not the

time nor place. Adele knows we loved her. It was a beautiful home going, and it smelled of nothing but magnolias throughout the building.

Someone else in the chapel sitting in the back captured my attention. He was young, like us. Everyone else was in their late 40s. Who was he? I tapped Abella and pointed to him. "Who is that?" I asked.

"His name is Murphy. But I don't know him, and no I have never met him," she responded.

I knew he was about 27 years old. I knew his name started with an "M," but I was thinking Matt, or Mike. Murphy? Yeah, he's definitely from the south. I pulled out my vintage mirror that looked like it had survived the Titanic and checked myself. Flawless. I looked at Abella. She already knew what I was about to do. He was handsome. Had light green eyes and sandy brown hair. It looked like he could pass for being mixed with black and white, I wasn't sure.

Abella rolled her eyes and gave me a head nod. I grabbed her hand as I put on my sexiest walk toward Murphy. You would think this was New York Fashion Week. I knew it wasn't the right place to spark a love interest, but hey … I was just introducing myself. Only dead fish go with the flow, and who knows? He could be my soul mate.

"Sorry to interrupt, you must be texting your girlfriend," I said to him when we walked up.

He laughed. Wow, his teeth were perfect too. Who is this guy, and why haven't I ever seen him around in a pub, or down at the crawfish market?

FOU by Angel Williams & Judith Jackson

"No, I don't have one of those," Murphy replied as I checked out the imprint in his pants.

"One of what?" I asked.

"A girlfriend …" Murphy responded with a confused look.

"OHHH! Yeah, I forgot, I mean, well …" I blushed. "Sorry, let me start over. Hi Murphy, my name is Summer," I said.

Abella nudged me in the back. Oh crap! I forgot he didn't tell me his name. He's going to think I'm some sort of creep, a stalker, or the CIA. I was hoping he didn't notice.

"How do you know my name?" Murphy asked as he stood up from the pew.

My eyes traced his body. He was about 6'3", lean, with a muscular body. Clearly, he worked out. He had a little bit of a beard growing back. *He must've shaved about four days ago,* I thought to myself.

"Oh … Ummm…" I tried to hurry up and think of an explanation.

"Your check stub, silly," Abella chimed in.

I looked down at the seat he was sitting in, and he did in fact have a check stub. The printing of his name was way too small for us to have been able to read it from so far away, but maybe he will fall for it.

"Oh, ha-ha. Wow, you girls have 20-20 vision," Murphy said with a laugh. *If only he knew,* I thought to myself. "Well, yes, my name is Murphy. Nice to meet you, Summer. You are beautiful," he said.

I smiled from ear to ear. He was just as gorgeous.

"And my name is Abella! Summer is my best friend, Abella said and stepped closer to him.

"Hi, Abella. You are very pretty too. Nice to meet you," he said politely, with so much respect.

I hoped Abella wouldn't mess this up for me. I mean, come on. She has a boyfriend. I guess Abella could read my mind, because she quickly stepped back.

"That's great. Best friends are hard to come by," he said. "I noticed that this is your friend's funeral," he continued. "I am very sorry for your loss. My mother passed away when I was sixteen from cancer ..." he stated and then was quiet for a moment. "I am twenty-seven now, and I miss her every day, but I believe she lives within me. That's how you have to think of your friend," he explained to us.

Bingo. I knew he was about 27 years old. "I am so sorry to hear that. I am sure your mother would be very proud of the man you have become." I spoke gently to him. He was masculine but had a soft nature about him. I hoped he would be able to handle me, if it even went that far. "What are you doing here? Did you know Adele?" I asked.

"No, I actually work here. I am the one who prepared your friend's body for her burial. I chose this job because of my mom. I always want to make sure the dead are handled with care."

Whoa. That was so deep and real. I was just thinking about how funeral parlors handle the dead. It was so weird how he was just answering all my questions. "That is beautiful," I told him. "I am Louisiana Creole, so I am more than adamant about the dead going peacefully and transitioning safely into their new life. If you don't mind me asking, what are you?"

"I'm human," he said with a grin. "No, I am also Louisiana Creole. Just French and Black though. No Indian or Spanish."

My thoughts were on point as always. I knew he was black and white. You could tell by the color of his eyes. Many full Louisiana Creoles get dark brown eyes from the Spanish trait. I ended up with light eyes. Creole is so beautiful. So many looks, but you know when someone is Creole. Whatever he was, he was beautiful.

"How about I take you to dinner, Summer? Do you like boudin, chitlins, and smoked sausage? I know this place an hour or so away called Billedeaux's, or we could go to Rabideaux's. We can grab some snow cones and hog cracklings for the drive."

"I would love to," I responded without hesitation.

He had said all the good food I loved and I loved to eat. Eating was an important part of my culture. It's where love comes from. Feeding someone you love means everything. It's good for your soul. Not that Louisiana Creole food was soul food, but it sure was good for the soul.

"How about six o'clock this Friday? We can hit the road right before sunset," I suggested.

Abella started tapping her foot. She was getting irritated, I could tell.

"It is a date."

We exchanged numbers. As he hugged me and said, "I will see you later," I felt my heart flutter. It was like a million butterflies in my stomach.

I was super excited to be going on a date with a man who seemed to have morals. *I really hope he can handle me,* I thought once again. He seemed patient and kind, and we had a lot in common already. I hope that he is my soul mate, so one day I can tell him about my power. I mean, after all, he is Creole.

"UHHHH HELLO!!! Earth to Summer!" Abella screamed.

"Girl, shhh! We are at a funeral!" I replied. Then I realized the whole chapel was empty, and Adele's casket was gone.

"No. We WERE at a funeral. The funeral is over! They already brought the casket down to the cemetery while you were too busy talking to Prince Charming to notice. What do you think this is? Princess and the Frog? Are you crazy?" Abella was going on a rant. I knew she was about to start speaking straight tongues.

"CALM DOWN!!!" I shouted. "You should be happy for me. I know Adele would be. I mean, she got beat into a coma by a horrible guy … she would be happy I met someone nice."

"Bullshit! That was disrespectful, and I don't even like Murphy. Something is weird about him! I got a bad feeling. He is Creole too. He is crazy, and I feel like he is a fraud. It's like he is wearing a mask! He belongs at Mardi Gras, the Grand Marshal of the whole damn parade! He is an act! A clown!" Abella screamed.

Here we go. Just like her to get jealous and upset that I am actually making room for a new relationship in my life. Just like she can read people, so can I, and I think he is awesome. She's going to have to chill out and let me live my own life, and make my own mistakes. Everyone has a destiny. I continued to let her rant as we walked out the chapel.

"Are you listening to me, Summer?" she asked while tapping me. "YES! I hear you, Abella. Please stop," I begged.

Her anger was getting worse, and right when we were about to pull out the parking lot of the chapel, a bird flew into our windshield. It's as if someone had splattered red paint on a painting at a painting class, and my car was the mural. The glass was completely covered with blood.

I looked at Abella. "Why did you have to go and do that? Look at what you did!" I screeched at her. "This poor bird!" I said as I pulled over.

"I didn't do it. I am trying to tell you something is not right about that man. And this was a sign."

She flashed her cocky little, smile as if she was telling me, "I told you so."

The truth of the matter is, I knew she didn't kill that bird. I knew it was an omen. But that doesn't mean it was an omen for me about Murphy. I mean, where was her boyfriend anyway? Why is she so concerned with my love life, when her own boyfriend didn't show up to Adele's funeral? What was HE doing? Abella can read everyone else, but not her own boyfriend. If that isn't strange, I don't know what is.

I kept my mouth shut, but I knew Abella was aware of what I was thinking. She didn't speak on it though because she knew I was right. The sun was getting closer to the ground and it had cooled off. I took a towel from the trunk of the car and gently wiped off the bird's remains. As I buried it in a little hole off the road, I instantly thought of Murphy. I bet he would've done the same thing. Rest in peace, little birdy.

Back in the car, I rolled down the windows and cut off the AC. I decided to enjoy the weather and daydream about the possibility of having found my soul mate as we headed to the cemetery to say our final goodbyes with a basket of water lilies to place on Adele's tombstone.

Chapter 12

Summer

Friday came quickly. Probably because I had been so excited. It was the end of May, and even in springtime, it's beyond hot down here in Louisiana. It was one of those states where you just couldn't beat the heat, no matter what.

My favorite seasons are autumn and summer, and not just because my name is Summer. Halloween is one of my favorite holidays. I don't know why I was even thinking about Halloween while getting ready for my date. It must be because Halloween is the only holiday you can dress up and be someone you're not. I mean, people pretend to be someone they're not all the time, but eventually their real selves are exposed. You can't hide who you really are, so I'm just going to be myself.

I kept thinking about how Abella said Murphy was wearing a mask. Did she see something that I didn't see in him? Perhaps could she read him? I know if I wanted to, I could have read Murphy, but that wouldn't be fair at all. He had gained my trust, and didn't deserve to have his privacy invaded.

I smiled at myself in the mirror as I applied the other wing of eyeliner to my eyes; I loved the cat eye look. Standing back, I checked myself out. Yeah, I was looking good. Trying not to be too sexy, I picked a pretty white summer dress to wear. Instead of the normal red lip, I did a baby pink.

"I look like a virgin," I said to myself.

Usually, I look like a vixen. I blew a kiss to my own reflection and prayed I didn't do anything weird tonight. It was 5:45 PM. Murphy said he would be here at 6:00. We had been texting all week since we met at Adele's funeral. He was far from boring, just how I liked it. I cracked my window to let in a breeze. The ceiling fan wasn't enough. I felt my anxiety starting to act up. What if he doesn't like me? Yeah, I am gorgeous … but I have a lot of ways. I do not want to end up loving this boy so much that I kill him by accident. It is possible to love somebody to death. Ughhhhh!

"Positive thoughts bring positive results," I said to my reflection. No matter how hard I tried to stop, my mind just kept on racing a million miles per second.

As soon as I laid down on my bed to watch the ceiling fan rotate, I heard a car engine pull up in the driveway. I jumped out of bed, sprayed on my favorite perfume, Estee' Lauder Youth Dew to be exact, and caught my breath as I walked to the door.

"Wow. You're looking more gorgeous than you did at the funeral," Murphy complimented me.

I was all smiles. He just knew the right things to say. "You too," I said with a grin, probably looking like

Cheshire Cat from Alice in Wonderland. How cheesy, I scolded myself. I mean, I just couldn't stop smiling.

I know he thinks I look even better because I am not wearing any lace stockings today. All he sees is yellow flesh. I was wearing a hat at the funeral, and my hair was pulled back into a bun. Now he sees my long curly locks. I flipped my hair over my shoulders and popped my leg, trying to be funny. It worked.

"You are quite the character, Ms. Summer," Murphy said as he took his hands from behind his back and handed me a bouquet of deep violet colored roses.

How different, I thought as I looked at the dark colored roses. I mean, they are pretty much black, and black roses aren't anything to be happy about. White roses would've been more appropriate. I looked down at my white dress and compared it to the black bouquet of flowers that looked like he'd grabbed them off someone's headstone on his way here.

"Aww, they are beautiful! Thank you! So different … But why black?" I asked, afraid of the answer. I couldn't stop thinking about what Abella had said.

"Well, black is not really a color. No color is really a color. Color does not exist. Black is all of the colors put together. It just depends on how the sun reflects off of it, and what part of the spectrum we are seeing it from." He watched for my reaction as he fixed his cufflinks.

I awkwardly stared at him for a few seconds as I tried to let his theory marinate in my mind. Lost in the loop, I offered a warm smile.

He looked different from the first time I met him. It was the end of May, hot as hell, and this man was dressed to impress in a black suit, a grey tie with little white polka dots, a white-collar shirt, and gold square cufflinks. He had a grey handkerchief in his chest pocket. I didn't know whether to be impressed by his answer and his choice of wardrobe or to run for the hills because this guy is clearly dressed for a court date, or a wake.

But then I realized I was different too. I replied, "Yes, color does not exist. That's why there is no slavery anymore, and all the plantations can have a peaceful evening."

Murphy smiled and held out his arm for me to take. We walked to the car and he even opened my door. Closed it too. I felt like a fine southern belle being pampered by my hard working husband. You don't find guys like this every day. Chivalry isn't dead afterall. I quickly gathered my thoughts and tried to not jump the gun so much. That's when it always goes wrong. You can't rush things, or force them to happen.

Murphy got in on the driver side and I could smell his cologne. It was a mix of Dolce and Gabanna, and I couldn't make out the other smell. He opened his glove compartment and pulled out a green bottle with a guy and a horse on the front. Oh, how did I not guess that? *Polo by Ralph Lauren, duh,* I said in my head. I waited for him to turn on the music so I could see what kind of guy he really was, but he didn't. I fiddled with my ankle bracelet out of nervousness.

"Don't be nervous, be excited. We are about to get snow cones for the drive, like I promised," Murphy said, breaking the silence. I didn't know I was being so obvious. This man was just too fine, and he wasn't nervous around me, which means he probably gets a lot of good looking' girls.

"Ok," I softy said.

We pulled up to the window of a popular neighborhood snow cone place called Mr. Snow. Wow, he even knew the hottest place to get snow cones. I couldn't believe I had never seen him before.

A heavyset woman with a hair net on her head came to the window. "How y'all dew-in? Whea y'all goin' all fancy like dat there? What y'all want a snow cone fo, lookin' like y'all goin' ta get married, chile." The woman chuckled as she spoke.

She instantly made us smile. That was that southern hospitality. I ordered a peach Louisiana crunch cake flavored snow cone. Murphy ordered a king cake flavor, and mixed it with a little pineapple. We tried each other's flavors and they were both delicious. It was really sexy how he would eat his snow cone lick his lips afterwards.

I thought about making love to him right then and there. In the car, in the heat, pulled off on a dirt country road, while our sweat dripped and intertwined with each other. The only thing cooling us down would be the ice melting from our snow cones. Let me stop. *This is a classy man,* I reminded my ego. We all know us Creole women have split personalities. The change in gears is what brought me back to reality. He was a fast driver. Even better.

We drove pretty much in silence all the way to the restaurant, just admiring the scenery. As nervous as I was, the silence proved we were comfortable around each other. However, it was obvious we both had more confidence through text messages. I don't know why. We both fine as hell.

The sun was setting over the road ahead of us, but it was bright enough to show a twinkle in his eyes. I thought he was perfect. After a few more miles, we finally arrived at Billedeaux's.

About forty-five minutes later, we were indulging into our food. I had spicy boudin balls with a crawfish platter. He had boiled shrimp with corn on the cob and boiled potatoes. Another thing we had in common was our love for hot sauce and seasoning because boy did we load it up. We both had MGDs to wash down the spices.

A little tipsy, I went to the jukebox. "What ya wanna hear?" I asked while clapping my hands. "AL GREEN!" he yelled. "NO! NO! The Temptations!!!" he added.

He definitely had an ear for good music. I picked a song and began to wind my hips.

"It was just my imaginationnnnn, runnin' away with meeeeee!!!" We both sang as he took my hands and twirled me around.

I was having the time of my life. It's as if we were reliving a past life, in the 70's or something. I loved it. He was very family oriented and had gone to many fish fries and yard boils as a child, just like me. That's how we knew these songs. Songs that really used to be played only by the jukebox or on records by a record player. It was like we were walking down a memory lane full of memories we had never even had together.

The songs brought back memories of my papa. He loved him some Temptations. When I was younger, he would be frying some crawfish, and while it was frying, we would dance around the kitchen and sing to each other. Moments with my papa were never dull. He took me to all the best fish fries and cookouts. He made the best lemonade. He was such a good father.

After a few more songs, Murphy urned to me and said, "Let's go and look at the stars."

I smiled and grabbed his arms as we ran to the car like two teenagers in love.

We hopped in and he drove about fifteen minutes down one of the darkest highways I had ever been on. We passed the bayou and crossed over many bridges. When we finally got to the destination, it was worth it. The sky was filled with beautiful stars, glistening like they were dancing millions of miles away at another party that we would never be invited to in this lifetime. We wouldn't be able to hear the song the stars were dancing to until we got there.

"You know, out of all these stars I see ... you're the brightest one," Murphy said as he looked in my eyes.

I felt my face getting red. I swear, he was everything that a woman could wish for. He did something to me. I was stuck in a trance that no spell could break. He definitely had to have the voodoo for me.

"So why is it that I have never seen you around anywhere, but you knew where the most crackin' snow cone spot was? Where have you been hiding?" I nudged him in his strong, cut shoulder.

"Well, I'm a hardworking man. I rarely go out, and if I do, it's to work. I had moved to Houston for a few years, maybe one day I will take you to Galveston. They have a sick beach, with many rides on the pier. They have a lot of snacks too … pecan pie, sweet potato … whatever you want. I see how fast you ate that snow cone," he said with a smile.

"I would love to. I am afraid of heights though, but I would definitely be down for some snacks."

"Why are you afraid of heights?" he asked.

"Well, they are just not good. Cats aren't afraid of heights, because they land on their feet. And even if they don't, they have nine lives. We as humans don't." I turned my head to look out the window, wondering if I should elaborate or not. I decided to. "Well, I mean … humans could have nine lives. I mean, we do. Just not as humans. And we have way more than lives. So, I guess I should not be afraid of heights. I could either land on my feet, or not. I'd still live though, just not in human form anymore," I stated.

He looked at me with tears in his eyes. I started to wonder what I said or did wrong, that caused this grown man to have tears in his eyes. "And that's what happened to my mom. She didn't land on her feet, but she gained wings because she didn't need her feet anymore. She's still living, just not in this world," he finished.

I took his hand and held it. We had a spiritual connection. I just hoped that I wouldn't run him away. I wanted to love him for myself, and give him the love his mother could no longer give him. I wanted to replace his hurt and pain with pure happiness and joy. I wanted to love him forever, until death do us part.

Chapter 13

Abella

I was devastated after my cousins' death. Depressed, filled with pure hatred. I hated the world. I hated every being in it. Yet, I had to learn how to live and cope with life. I couldn't make life harder than it already was. After isolating myself from the world for months, I decided to get back in tune with life. My heart yearned for life. I wanted to live, live a normal life at that. I wanted to love and to be loved. I wanted to have a family, I wanted it all … but I had no idea how to maintain or accept the things I wanted. Like they say, old habits were hard as heck to break …

I sat on the couch all alone in my apartment, staring at the blank television. My world had been turned upside down since the death of Adele. I still wasn't able to quite grasp the fact that my cousin was no longer here with us. I just couldn't accept the reality that I would never see her cherubic face again, hear her beautiful laugh, listen to all the advice that she gave me. Everything had just been taken away from me.

To make matters even worse, the friendship between Summer and me had deteriorated. Things with us just weren't the same anymore. We barely talked to each other, let alone saw one another. She was so far in love. At times, her head would be so far up Murphy's rectum, I couldn't tell where her body began.

Despite the way I was feeling, I forced myself up. It was time to do something about my life. I got up and got dressed in a black tulle skirt and a pink top. I brushed lip gloss across my lips, and wore my naturally curly hair out. I was tired of being cooped up in the house, dying in my own misery.

I called Summer's phone a few times, but she didn't answer. She rarely answered me. Every time I talked to her, it was an 'I will call you back' or something like that. She either didn't have time for me or she was busy, let her tell it.

I had called her earlier, but she said she was in bed sick. I was hoping she felt a little better now, so we could go out for a walk and have a long well needed talk.

Instead, it was me, my lonesome self and I tonight. Well, I'd had enough, I was going to go out and enjoy myself by myself. There was a time to live and a time to die, and this was my time to live.

———————

I parked my car in front of the bar and got excited about having a bit of entertainment. I hadn't been out since the night Adele disappeared. A part of me felt guilty for having any kind of fun, while Adele lay trapped in the cemetery. If only I had kept a closer watch on her, maybe she would still be here.

In a matter of hours, I was sloppy drunk and all over the place. The bartender took my car keys and told me he was calling me a cab to get home. As soon as he turned his head, I slipped out the bar. My night wasn't over just yet.

As I walked the dark streets of New Orleans, the honking of a horn caused me to jump a bit. When I turned around, I saw a very handsome guy. He didn't become familiar until I heard his voice.

"Come get in the car. It's too dangerous to be out here by yourself," he yelled out to me.

"You fine, but you ain't that fine. I'm good." I waved him off.

"Fine, then I'll walk with you," he said and parked his car.

When he got out the car, I smiled at his overall appearance. He was tall and very sexy. From the first time I met him, I always thought he was so damn fine.

"If you don't mind getting wet." I smiled.

A few seconds later, the rain began to pour down on us.

"How did you know it was going to rain?" he asked as he dodged for cover, grabbing me with him.

I smiled at him as the two of us stood in front of a store. "I know everything," I joked.

"What's your name?" he asked.

"Abella, and what's yours?" I questioned.

"Nice to meet you, Abella. I'm Dylan."

"Well, Dylan, don't you know this is our second time meeting?" A part of me hoped that he remembered me.

"Duh, I remember exactly who you are, Abella. I was just joking with you. How could I forget you with that beautiful face?"

I stared at him and smiled again. I couldn't help but to smile at his handsome self. Already, he was making my heart skip a beat; the butterflies in my stomach began to softly dance.

In his eyes, I could see the lust. "Well, I'll see you around, Dylan." I said as I backed into the rain and headed down the street.

I was just about to cross the street when I saw Summer and Murphy eating at my favorite restaurant. They were all smiles, and seemed to be lost in each other. I could tell it was love. This man was taking my best friend from me. I was a bit jealous, and I couldn't help but to say something to her. Before I could stop myself, I had stormed through the doors of the restaurant.

When Summer saw my face, it was priceless. Last time I talked to her she didn't feel well. Now here she was all lovey dovey.

"Summer, I thought you were sick," I said as I stood at her table.

She jumped up from her seat and grabbed my arm.

"What is it? Why are you treating me like this? What did I do to you?" I asked Summer as she pulled me to the front of the restaurant.

She stared out the door for a second. "You didn't do nothing wrong, Abella. It's just..."

"It's just what?" I cut her off. "There's no excuse for the way you have been treating me lately. I've been calling you, I've been texting you. You been ignoring me, and then you say you are sick, and here you are all lovey dovey!"

I could feel myself getting angrier with each word. I hated the fact that Summer always stood and lied in my face, as if I didn't know she was telling me a damn lie. Or was it that she actually didn't care? I hated liars and she knew that. Why couldn't she just tell me the truth. Didn't I deserve the truth?

"Abella, it's just that I want a different way of living. I want to try something new. I want to forget about our gifts, and just do something different for once," she expressed.

"And does that something different not involve me?" I rolled my eyes as I waited for her to answer.

She sighed then looked out the door again. "No, it doesn't involve you, Abella. Sometimes you get really upset and you cause a lot of trouble. You don't want the same thing as I want anymore. I think we've outgrown each other. You will always be like a sister to me, I just need space at the moment, and I need to find myself."

"What the hell do you mean? After all we have been through?" I yelled.

"See, this is the problem. I want no parts of this," Summer stated.

People stopped eating and began to watch us. I didn't care one bit.

"I hate you, Summer!" I said through gritted teeth.

I sent a harsh slap across her cheeks.

"I hate you even more. I always hated you," she shot back with tears in her eyes. "I hate your guts, Abella, you are fou! Freaking crazy!"

My heart cringed at her words. I began to get hot, and I stared at her hard. I could feel myself losing control. Summer stared back at me, and I saw no fear. She was ready for whatever I was about to throw at her.

"You throw a shot and I will throw an even harder one back. This isn't Abella's world!" she said.

I turned around and ran out the restaurant. As I stumbled down the street, I ran right into Dylan, who was waiting outside the restaurant for me.

"Are you okay?" he asked as I fell into his waiting arms.

I shook my head no and he helped me into his car. I'd lost my favorite cousin, and now here I was losing my best friend. Why? Because I was slightly different from the rest. I couldn't change the things that I truly had no control over.

Dylan turned the music on and drove down the streets. I was very grateful for his concern, and I felt safe

and comfortable with him. His eyes, spoke a song that I
wanted to understand. At that moment, I felt like I wanted
to get to know him, all of him.

Chapter 14

Summer

It was a beautiful autumn day, and Murphy and I sat on the front porch eating pumpkin pie and watching some of the leaves slowly fall off the trees to their death. In Louisiana we didn't get much of a change in season, so for Halloween, we took a road trip to Savannah to get the full affect. Being near the water gave us the crisp fall feeling that every soul deserves to feel. We even got to admire the color change of the leaves. Reds, oranges, and deep purples, as if the tree was having its very own sunset, a funeral, preparing for the chilly winter.

"Are you happy we didn't wear a costume?" Murphy asked me.

"Yes. I'd much rather us be ourselves with each other, no need to disguise who we really are," I replied.

At the mention of costumes, my mind wandered back to when Abella and I used to go trick-or-treating. Ashamed of who we were, we impatiently waited for Halloween to come around. We would get dressed up in costumes and run the city all night long, having a blast, with no worries and cares in the world. No one knew our real identity under the masks that we wore. At one point in my life, I wished everyday was Halloween, so I could hide the identity that had been forced upon me.

I still felt a little bad about our argument. Some of the things I said were out of anger and frustration. Of course I didn't hate Abella, I was just tired. She was content to live her life in misery and hatred, but I did not want that for myself. I needed to be and do better. Murphy was taking all my pain and anger and replacing it with love. I loved my friend, but I needed a break. We were toxic together, and we needed to learn how to have control and balance in our lives. Our friendship was like a shrimp boat. At one time it was great, out in the bayou floating perfectly fine. But then the boat got a hole. And every day, our friendship sank. Little by little, more water poured in. I really hoped our friendship would stand the test of time. But like I was taught, only time would tell.

———————

Winter rolled around, and Murphy and I were still going strong. He always managed to keep me warm. The two of us had a magical connection like no other. It was far from an illusion, it was really love. Making love to him was like a blazing flame inside a fireplace during a snowy day. Our lives were picture perfect, just the two of us and our everlasting love. We dedicated the holidays to family time. I didn't have much family, so our holidays were always spent with his family.

The first Christmas we spent with his family was the best gift ever for me. I fit in perfectly. They welcomed me with open arms. It was the family that I never had. Murphy was a bit sad about his mother's absence.

Although it had been over a decade since cancer had taken her life, he still missed her terribly. The kisses we shared under the mistletoe helped his mood a bit. I didn't expect any gifts. The love and time he gave me was more than enough.

Murphy walked through the double doors of his family's antique house carrying a cream colored box with a big red bow sitting on top of it, looking like a bunch of poinsettias. The priceless smile painted on his face said he was up to something. When he set it down, the box started to move. I immediately thought to myself, *this man must be a magician. How is he making the box move by itself?*

"Open it," he told me with an excited grin on his face.

I crept a bit closer to the box and realized it wasn't sealed shut, and it had holes under the red ribbon. As I removed the top, a puppy jumped into my arms and covered my face with wet kisses. I was so happy. It was a cairn terrier, like the dog in *The Wizard of Oz*. My heart melted as I stared into the puppy's big bright eyes.

"Well, what are you going to name her?" Murphy asked me. "Pansy, yup, that's her name. Pansy like a beautiful flower," I replied.

"Let's see what else I got for you," Murphy stated.

His family all stood up. Murphy grabbed Pansy out of my hands and handed her over to one of his little cousins. He pulled out a black cloth. "Go ahead and turn around," he told me.

I hesitated at first, then I turned around with a face full of smiles. Normally, I would trust no one to blindfold me, but ever since my heart started dancing to the beat of Murphy's heart, I trusted him. He grabbed my hand and led me outside the house. Although it was Christmas, it was somewhat warm and felt like it could have been spring. The fresh scent of nature filled my nostrils, flowers and dandelions started to take the place of the grasslands. The moss trees had gained back their heavy coats, and cotton flew through the wind.

He slowly eased the cloth off my face. "Oh my, Murphy! Did you get this for me?"

I rushed over to the gold convertible that Murphy had surprised me with.

"Just as the butterflies are fluttering, you should do the same. Because you are much like a butterfly. Beautiful, and hard to catch," Murphy told me.

He knew the way to my heart. All the right words, he spoke them to me. His charming smile always melted my heart.

"Thank you, Murphy." I blushed. "But what does a convertible have to do with a butterfly?" I asked.

"Now you can drop the top and fly through the wind as well," he said as he placed the keys in my hand.

I turned around and gave him a big hug then rushed off to check out my brand new car.

"Murphy, thank you!"

I smiled as I slid into the driver seat of my new car. I felt bad that I didn't get Murphy much for Christmas but a watch and a couple of sweaters. Soon, I was going to make that up to him and give him something that no other woman had ever given him.

_____

    Summer came and pushed spring right out the way. We took a trip to Galveston, just like he said we would. Murphy was a man of his word; what he spoke is exactly what he meant. His promises were never broken, that's one of the things I loved so much about him.

    The two of us had so much fun in Galveston. I wore a cowgirl hat and leather boots, and I was able to convince Murphy to wear a pair of leather cowboy boots along with a matching cowboy hat. We appeared to be the most perfect and loving couple to grace the earth.

    We did all sorts of exciting things. We got our hands dirty with BBQ turkey legs at the pier. Murphy helped me with my fear of heights, and we rode every roller coaster and kissed during the drops. The roller coaster was like our love, fast, and going higher with no regrets. When it got dark, the waters by the pier disappeared into the night, only to be replaced by flickering carnival lights from the rides. We could hear children's laughter, and the smell of popcorn, cotton candy, and funnel cakes filled the air.

    We walked the pier grounds hand in hand. "I am about to go play that game and win you a prize," Murphy told me while pointing to a dart range.

    I smiled and took a seat on a nearby bench. I watched as he tried and tried. He was a sore loser, so he wasn't going to give up until he won me something, as he'd promised.

When he came back, he was holding a huge pink kangaroo. "I told you I was going to win you something," he said as he handed it to me.

"Yeah, it took you like fifty bucks, but I love it, Murphy," I said.

"Well, that's not the prize," he told me. "The prize is you." He pointed to the kangaroo's pouch.

As I dug my hand in its pouch, I felt something dainty. It was jagged. As I pulled out the object, the carnival lights became irrelevant, because what I was holding in my hand shined much brighter. It was a ring. A beautiful diamond ring with a gold band.

When I looked back up, Murphy was already down on his knees, as a man should be when he's found his soul mate and wanted to take it to the next level.

"You are my prize. You are the woman I've been waiting for, for what felt like a lifetime. You are my other half, most importantly my better half. Will you marry me, Summer?" Murphy asked.

My heart literally stopped for a moment. I saw my future, and my future was him. People who were walking past stopped to catch a glimpse of the beautiful romantic moment. Tears flowed down my cheeks as I covered my mouth. Everything was just so perfect.

"YES!! Of course I will marry you!" I screamed.

As soon as we kissed, just as in the movies, fireworks went off. Happy Fourth of July.

Chapter 15

Summer

Although my friendship with Abella was slowly fading away, like a ship sailing out to sea, becoming more distant, and then completely invisible as it went into the fog, I was super excited to tell her about Murphy's proposal. I had to tell someone about my terrific news. I pulled out the picnic basket filled with goat cheese, chicken salad sandwiches, pears, and caramel-coconut candy and placed the plaid tan and red blanket right underneath the biggest willow tree I could find. *Perfect!* I thought.

As soon as I sat down, I saw Abella. It was like she just appeared out of nowhere. I was hesitant at first, and thought twice about inviting her. Abella just wasn't the same as she used to be. Perhaps it was Adele's death. I wasn't sure what it was. Truthfully, I missed the old Abella, my old friend.

"Hey," I said, almost scared as I stood to my feet.

"Hello," she replied and sat down across from me. I pulled out the snacks and she immediately went for the candy.

I stared at her for a few seconds.

"Don't look at me like that," she stated, not once looking up at me. I knew she was feeling my presence as she always did. She was always able to feel a person's presence.

"I don't know where our friendship is going, but I love you. I don't care what has happened in the past. We can't change that. We only have the future," I started. "It's time for us to leave the crazy behind. We are getting older, and we cannot control fate and destiny. We are not supposed to play God—" I said.

"OH PLEASE, someone bring out the violins!" Abella interrupted. It was just like her. She was set in her old rude ways.

"Well... Abella," I said. I couldn't find the right words to tell her I was a fiancée. So instead, I held out my hand, which showed my ring, sparkling in the 3 PM daylight. "I would love for you to be my maid of honor."

Abella looked at the ring and then looked at me, and then back at the ring. "I think you're stupid," she scolded me. "You don't even love him, he doesn't even love you. Love isn't real. Emotions and feelings change. Something is wrong with that man!" she screamed.

I shook my head. Typical thing for her to say. It was funny though, she's been with Dylan for a while now, and she still can't read him. How did she know he loved her? She had admitted in one of our few conversations since our incident at the restaurant that Dylan was unreadable.

"Does Dylan love you?" I asked with my hands folded across my chest. "Is it real, Abella, or is it magic? Just like a damn illusion!"

"It's real! And if it wasn't, I don't care." Abella hissed.

I knew she was lying, I could see it all over her face. Because she was uncertain that her love was real, she had to just rain on my parade. But it wasn't going to happen today. Before we got into a heated argument, I decided to calm down a bit.

"Abella, I am in love. He is in love with me. We are happy. In the past year, he has made me realize what life was truly about. And it's about living. Not dying. I am going to marry him," I firmly stated.

Abella stood up, stepping on some of the sandwiches. "Well, Summer, this is goodbye. You picked him over me. I thought we were best friends until the end of time. Maybe this is the end of OUR time. I will not be your maid of honor, because you are not honorable. You fell in love with a bastard and pushed me to the side. Now I must do the same to you. You're dead to me," she said, looking right into my eyes.

I stood up gracefully. "Abella, you are being crazy. You can still be my friend until the end of time. I can't have babies with you or build a family with you. Hell, I don't want to make love to you. You are acting more like you are crazy in love with me instead of being my friend and genuinely loving me as a friend." As I spoke, I started to realize that maybe she had more feelings for me than I thought. "You have to understand..." I started, but she cut me off.

"I understand completely. You are leaving me for a man you will regret leaving me for. He is nothing, and I am everything. I am a woman. When he starts beating you and cheating on you, don't call me. There won't be a need to say I TOLD YOU SO. You have the same gift as me. You are trying to hide your roots to be a housewife. You are not strong, and you should be ashamed to represent Creole. You're just a basic, not special at all!" She screamed at me. "Good luck! You'll need it! Karma is a bitch!" She screamed at me while walking away. Her face was red and her eyes were filled with tears. She was angry and hurt.

"Oh, and Abella ..." I called out after her. "Your love with Dylan isn't real. It's magic, and when it backfires, you'll reap what you sowed. You should have stopped playing with fire years ago as you were told many times. Oh, and speaking of karma, you will definitely meet that bitch."

I meant every word. I could read Abella from miles away. I wished no bad luck upon her, but I couldn't stop it either. What she had coming for her, no man or woman on earth could stop it.

She turned around and stared at me for a second. I could see the pure hate that lingered in her eyes. "Don't test me. EVER!" She screamed.

I didn't try to stop her as she stormed off. When Abella is in that mood, it is very dangerous. I did fear for her life though. She was capable of hurting anyone, even herself. I looked down at my ring, and the hurtful words she said to me faded away. I was happy. Ready to move on to a new chapter of my life.

Sweet juices dripped down my chin as I took a bite out of the pear. I looked up at the willow tree as some of its beauty drifted and swayed back and forth in the summer breeze. Life is a lot like a tree. Although parts of it may die, other parts continue to grow, as long as the foundation is strong. Murphy and I had built a strong foundation, and even though my friendship with Abella had just died, I know my other relationships will continue to grow, as they should.

Chapter 16

Abella

I couldn't believe the nerve of Summer! Then, for her to think that I wanted her as more than a friend. Who did she really think she was? It was in a woman's nature to think once or twice about another woman. Every woman had thought about another one before, and if they said they didn't, they were lying. But I loved Summer in a different type of a way. I loved her as a friend. I was envious when others came in the picture. She was my Summer. It was crazy for me to say, but yes, I wanted her all to myself. I wanted to protect her and love her as a friend should. But she couldn't see that.

Instead, she looked as me if I was crazy and dangerously in love with her. As if I had no balance or control in my life, she looked at me as if I was a threat and danger to myself and everyone around me. She acted as if she didn't once see the person I truly was. The loving and caring friend for a lifetime. The fun we used to have, the jokes we used to tell each other. When the world turned against the two of us, we were all we had and wanted. Now it was nothing, just mere memories.

I walked through the woods to Dylan's house. I needed to talk to him, most importantly, I needed to feel his hot body next to mine. He seemed to be the only one able to calm me down when I was heated.

Walking up Dylan's stairs, I let out a bunch of tears that were hopelessly fighting to be freed. I wiped my tears and knocked on the door a few times. When I didn't get an answer, I looked and noticed that his car wasn't parked outside.

Frustrated tears built up in my eyes yet again. I never had anyone when I truly needed someone. With a sigh, I sat on his porch and patiently waited for him. The sun began to hide, and before I knew it, the moon had come out of hiding. I was mad that I left my cell phone at home on the charger. I had no way of calling Dylan, and I dreaded that long walk home.

Finally, after what felt like an eternity, Dylan's car pulled up. I yawned as I stood up and walked to his car. I was beyond furious.

"Where were you?" I questioned Dylan, trying hard not to be the overly aggressive and possessive girlfriend that no one wanted.

Dylan looked at me as if I was crazy. "Are you okay, Abella?" he asked with concerned eyes.

"No, I'm not okay. I been sitting here waiting on you for hours. Where have you been?" I asked again.

I stared into his eyes to see if they told a story that could be read. They didn't. They never told me anything. At times it pissed me off that I wasn't able to read Dylan. Who was protecting him, and why? He was the first person I had wanted to read and wasn't able to do so. When we lay in bed after a long night of giving ourselves to each other, he would peacefully fall asleep, and I would grab his palms and try to see what he was all about. I always came up empty.

"Did you forget that I have a job? That I have to work? Did that ever cross your mind?" Dylan asked as if he was annoyed by the fact that I was questioning him.

I turned my nose up and trailed behind him as he entered the house.

"I'm just having a bad day. I got into yet another heated argument with Summer. I think this time it's really the end of our friendship," I stated as I sat down on his love seat.

"You two act as if you are more so dating than friends. Let bygones be bygones. You are outgrowing each other. When are y'all going to accept that, and stop with all the nonsense?"

"What's your problem? Why are you talking to me like this, Dylan?" I questioned.

I reached over and grabbed his hands. He normally would snatch his hands away from me. This time, he allowed me to proceed with my doings.

"Abella, will you ever act normal? Just because you have a gift does not mean you need to use it at all times. I didn't sign up for all of this," he said.

I closed my eyes, and just as always, I got nothing from him. Nothing at all.

"I'm covered by the voodoo queen." He laughed as he got up and stormed off upstairs.

I ran behind him. "Dylan is everything okay between us?"

As he took off his shirt, his chiseled body had me craving and lusting for him. I licked my lips as I thought about the way he made me feel so good. Like I was the only woman he ever wanted or needed. Then all of a sudden, everything just stopped. As if he didn't care for me as much anymore. Maybe it was my craziness that was driving him insane. Maybe my gift was scaring him away.

"We are fine. I'm just going through some things, and my momma has not been well."

"Your momma?"

"Yes," he replied.

"I thought your momma was—" I began, but stopped before the word deceased came out my mouth. I actually didn't know much about his momma; he never mentioned her.

"No, she's not. She's well. I see her, but not as often as I'd like."

"Why haven't I ever met her?" I was a bit jealous. Why hadn't he ever taken me home to his momma?

Dylan turned to face me. He stared me up and down. The look in his eyes, I didn't like one bit. He was looking at me as if I was nobody, as if I was worthless. The same looks that people throughout the town used to give Adele and me.

"You are so selfish, you never once asked about her. All you have been doing is prancing around, talking about you and Summer. I'm tired of you two. You two should get together. You belong together," he said, while shaking his head. He walkedg around the room and I trailed right behind him.

"Don't you dare say that!" I began to get angry. "Where is your momma at? I want to meet her now!"

Dylan snatched his bath towel from his bedroom closet. "You won't meet her."

"And why not!" I yelled as I sat on the edge of the bed to calm myself down a bit. I could already see things were getting out of control.

Dylan ignored my question as he made his way to the bathroom.

I raced over to him and snatched the towel out of his hand. "Why not?" I demanded.

"Because she doesn't like your kind." He spoke with force while staring into my eyes. He snatched the towel from me and left me standing outside of the bathroom door, hurt and lost in my own thoughts. What did he mean by she didn't like my kind? Who was she to judge me and not know me?

I waited an hour outside the bathroom door for Dylan. I wanted to know exactly what he meant by his momma not liking my kind.

Dylan opened the door and stepped out with his towel wrapped around his waist. The light from the bathroom lightly lit the dark house. When he turned the bathroom light off, the house went dark again.

"What do you mean by my kind?" I asked.

I could hear the panic in Dylan voice as he flicked on the hallway light. "Abella, what are you doing? Are you crazy?"

"Did I scare you?" I let out a wick laugh.

"Never." He shook his head and went into the bedroom.

"I think it's time for you to leave."

I stood in front of him, staring for a minute or so.

"You'll regret how you treated me, Dylan," I said before storming downstairs to grab my belongings.

I had to gain some sort of control to keep my Dylan. It was the two of us forever. We were meant to be, we were meant to love one another forever and ever. Til' death do us part was how it was supposed to be, and how it was going to be.

Chapter 17

Summer

Murphy and I wanted a small, intimate wedding. We chose a small country town in Iota. Acadia Parish, to be exact. After my argument with Abella, I made myself busy with planning the wedding. I chose canary yellow and white for the colors. An outside wedding, because nature and the universe play a big role in our lives. I tried on many dresses during the end of the summer before I finally fell in love with a certain one. It was lace, with a long train. The veil I chose sat delicately on top of a diamond crown. I felt like a princess.

The day had finally arrived. Late August, early autumn. Indian summer. The cake with its three tiers sat beautifully under the rope lights that wrapped around all the moss trees. It was white, and looked like a wedding dress itself. The candles burned, giving off a warm tinkling glow from inside the crystal glasses. The silverware and china were spotless and waiting to be filled with delectable southern food. For the first time in years, I allowed vodka around me. Bowls of iced tea and lemonade were spiked with the devil's juice. We called the drinks a firefly. Soft jazz played as I nervously waited for the wedding music to start. I was about to walk down the aisle.

I never saw this day coming, but I had always hoped it would. I was sad that Abella wouldn't be there. Dylan did not attend of course, because Abella would've cut his tongue out of his mouth with one swipe of her hand if he dared. My family members as well as some of Murphy's filled the satin seats with big canary yellow bows on the back of them. Everything was perfect. I placed the veil over my face as I heard the organs start. Gracefully, I walked through the grass, trying not to fall.

Murphy looked so handsome. He stood there in a white suit, a canary yellow tie, and white leather shoes. The yellow daffodil in his pocket, neatly placed in front of the canary handkerchief, like the ones he always had. His gold cuff links shined almost as bright as his white teeth. He does. And I do.

After the ceremony, we feasted on all the delicious food. I kicked off my white heels and danced with him under the starry skies. Everyone was tipsy and enjoying themselves.

I picked up my bouquet. "Ok y'all, here it goes!"

Everyone gathered behind me. I tossed my bouquet and it landed near all the wedding gifts. No one caught it. All the ladies ran to the bouquet. They tore it all apart, each lady taking a flower or two. I guess everyone was next to get married. I giggled. I was the happiest woman alive. It's as if no one mattered but Murphy and I. We packed the wedding gifts up in the white Cadillac and thanked everyone for coming. As we drove away, I blew kisses to everyone. Murphy honked his horn.

As we departed, I knew some of the guests were reading the back of his window, which said, "UNTIL DEATH DO US PART," which was written in white frosting from the delicious cake.

Chapter 18

Abella

I didn't feel bad about not attending Summer's stupid wedding. I would've destroyed it anyway. All she cares about is her stupid husband anyway. I sat on my porch fanning myself down with a straw hat. The Indian summer heat couldn't possibly be as hot as the steaming blood running through my veins. Part of me wanted to do something terrible to Murphy. I would never hurt Summer. As mad as I am at her, deep down, I still have some feeling for her. I wouldn't say love, because it isn't real.

Dylan walked out the screened in part of the porch to join me outside. "We have to talk," he said. "This relationship isn't going anywhere. You are focusing way too much on Summer and Murphy. If that was really your friend, you would be happy for her," Dylan stated.

He leaned forward, placing his hands in front of his face. As strong as my powers were, I couldn't read Dylan. I tried over and over again. I even tried to do magic on him while he was sleeping one night, but I still couldn't read him. But in this case, I didn't have to. I could tell where the conversation was going, and I didn't like it. He was about to leave me.

"Dylan, I'm so sorry. Let me make dinner for you, and we can discuss this further. I know you are hungry, baby," I said, scooting my chair closer to his.

"Abella, it isn't going to work. My feelings have changed. You are always so angry. It's like we are staying in the same place, and not growing at all. I don't want to be with you anymore. It isn't fun like it used to be, it's like a job. I don't even think you really love me or know what love is, or how to even love someone."

He was right about one thing. I did not love him. I was more so obsessed with him. I liked to control him. I liked having someone there. I didn't exactly know what love was, I only knew lust. But one thing about it, he was not about to leave me. Summer had already left me. Adele had left me too. I refused to be left again by anyone.

"Dylan, I completely understand where you are coming from," I said in a manipulative manner. "Let me feed you, and we can figure out what to do from here. I know you can't say no to red beans and rice, oxtails, cornbread, apricot pie and half and half, now can you?"

Dylan laughed, then he stopped. "I definitely can't say no to that, Abella. But after we eat, I am going to pack up my things from here. I have already been looking for a new spot. I am not happy here anymore." Dylan responded with his voice shaking.

"Come on inside and relax, while I prepare dinner." I walked into the cool house, leaving the autumn heat outside.

I prepared the meal. The house smelled delicious. It was so much food, you would think an army was about to pass through for a bed and breakfast. I set out the meal on the dining room table and lit candles to reflect off the chandelier that hung above it. I filled our glasses with half lemonade, and half iced tea. An Arnold Palmer is what it's called.

Before I called Dylan to the table, I walked back into the kitchen and stood over the apricot pie. I took a capsule from my apron pocket and gently sprinkled some over half of the pie. The same rosemary, ginger, and crushed rose petals I had put in his plate of food. He wouldn't be able to tell. I used Lawry's and Cayenne pepper to hide the taste and smell of my extra ingredients. I had concocted a love spell. Dylan would not be leaving me anytime soon.

"Dylan! Dinner is ready!" I yelled.

He rushed to the table. Poor guy was hungry. I haven't been cooking much. I *was* too worried about Summer. He didn't hesitate to start devouring the food.

"Like I said, Abella, I think it's time for me to move on …" Dylan stopped mid-sentence after the seventh or eighth bite. He started coughing and reached for his glass, but his hands were shaking too much to focus. He knocked it over and the broken glass cut his finger. *Perfect,* I thought. I needed some of his blood to finish the spell.

Dylan grabbed his throat, gasping for air. I sat there, eating my dinner. *Hmmm... could've used a little more sugar in the corn bread,* I thought. Dylan fell to the ground and immediately went to sleep. After I was done eating, I cleared the table. In the kitchen, I slit my wrist. I took his blood off the broken glass and mixed it with mine in a small porcelain bowl. "Ashes to ashes, dust to dust. To love forever, in just we trust. To be madly in love, forever until, one of us dies, or one of us kills."

I repeated it three times, smearing our mixed blood all over my face. Did the same thing to Dylan's face. I dragged his body to our bed and lay beside him. When he wakes up, he will not remember what happened, or him even wanting to leave. He was here to stay.

Dylan slept peacefully through the night as I watched him. When the sun started to rise, I washed both of our faces off with a warm washrag and burned the bloody cloth in the back of the house.

Chapter 19

Abella

I was so sick of not getting any phone calls from Summer.
Regardless of our falling out, we were still supposed to
be in contact with each other. After all, we were a team.
It's like she didn't care at all about me since that boy
came into her life. I didn't feel bad at all about what I was
about to do.

I put on my innocent face as I headed through the
doors of the funeral home Murphy worked at. I knew he
was at work today. No services were going on, but I
could smell death throughout the building. There he was.
He had gloves on so, I assumed he was working on
getting bodies ready for their home going.

"Hi Murphy, how are you today?" I asked said from
behind him. He looked startled.

"Wow! Hi, Abella. I haven't heard from or seen you
in a long time. Sorry about taking your best friend!" He
said, smiling, and laughing.

I knew he was joking, but it was far from a joke to
me. He would find that out during the rest of his shift
though.

"Oh, it's okay. I know you all are in love. I can't do for her what you do for her," I said, nearly choking on my words.

"What can I do for you today?"

"I wanted to see some bouquets of flowers you all offer. I want to surprise my boyfriend. Not with just flowers, but I'm going to make him an amazing meal and want to actually decorate the house full of beautiful, good scents that will go along with the wonderful food," I said, smiling.

"That's really sweet. Sure, hold on I will get you a brochure," he said and walked out the room. He left his jug of water behind.

I slipped in some pollen, ginger, and mustard seeds. It wasn't a clear jug, so he was going to drink it automatically. He wouldn't see a thing.

"Dance with the devil, sting your heart, make your world, fall apart. The dead is alive and the alive is dead, and for one more night, souls tap dance on Murphy's head!" I mumbled and stood up straight.

"Here you go, Abella. Whenever you decide which ones you want, come back in and I will put them together for you," Murphy said, looking handsome as ever, I must admit. Yuck.

"Thanks so much! I have to be running along now. Tell Summer I said hi!" I said over my shoulder as I rushed out the front door.

I knew it was about to go down in there. After Murphy waved goodbye to me and turned around, I ran to the back of the funeral home, up to the balcony, back in the main room. I had to see this!

Murphy picked up his jug and took a big gulp. Immediately, he knew it tasted different, I could see it in his face, but I am sure he had figured it was just his imagination from his hard work. He went in the back to continue embalming the bodies, preparing them for their families to see them and say goodbye for the last time. It was about 8 o'clock, and he was running behind since he'd stopped to give me flower advice. He was the only one there, or so he thought.

It was beyond hot inside the building, even though the sun had set. I was getting more excited for what was about to happen.

All of a sudden, an organ started playing. Here we go! I could sense everything he was thinking.

He figured someone had left the radio on, until he saw from the crack underneath the door that all the lights were on in the main room where funeral services are held.

"Maybe my boss forgot something," he told himself. He opened the door, and as soon as he did, he heard laughter.

I ducked down to get an even better view. The laughter was moving, as if a ton of people were running in circles around him giggling, but he couldn't see anyone, yet. That's when he saw it. Someone WAS sitting at the organ.

He wiped his eyes, and squinted harder. "HELLO?" He yelled. The person didn't respond. In fact, they started to play the organ louder, faster, harder. The laughing continued. As soon as Murphy got directly behind the person at the organ, the person stopped playing.

Murphy reached out to tap his shoulder. "Excuse me, sir, no one is allowed …" Before he could finish, the "person" at the organ turned around. He had no face, but a twisted skull, which looked like a black hole, a tunnel that directed everyone into another dimension, the afterlife. Murphy immediately recognized the old 1940's suit. It was one of the bodies he had worked on a few hours ago.

In shock, Murphy turned around and ran to the door. I had made sure the doors were all locked. The body didn't chase him. I made it go back to playing the organ. This time, jazz horns and trumpets accompanied him. Murphy banged on the doors. They were not budging. It was like a million people were leaning against the door, preventing his exit. He was stuck. The laughing got louder.

All the other bodies he had worked on earlier that day marched out in a single file line, walking through the walls of the church. Just as he'd heard, they were playing jazz horns and trumpets. It sounded as if a whole traditional New Orleans funeral was coming down Bourbon. The laughing got louder, the lights started flickering, and the bodies kept marching closer. The body on the organ started singing to his playing.

"Awwww, yeah yeah! Lonely souls, awwww yeah yeah, where do they go? Awwww, yeah, yeah, nobody knows until you cross to the other side, and when death comes for you, ya can't hide. Awww yeah yeah, lonely souls!"

Murphy looked like he was going crazy. The chaos seemed to last forever, even for me. I loved it. The bodies all had no face and they were dancing, singing, playing instruments around him. Murphy started crying and begging for mercy. "PLEASE STOP!! PLEASE GO REST IN PEACE! LET ME BE!!!" Murphy was now down on his knees, trembling and shaking.

They didn't stop. They kept going, getting louder and louder, lights still flickering. Then as abruptly as it had started, the body stopped playing the organ. The other bodies followed him and stopped. They all faced Murphy and pointed to him. A strange noise emitted from their mouths. Like fingernails scratching the inside of a coffin. Murphy covered his ears. It got worse. It was the sound of dying souls.

Every light bulb in the funeral home started to burst and explode one by one. When the final light exploded, leaving Murphy in complete darkness, the funeral home doors opened. He ran to his car, started the engine, and sped out the parking lot. He had just witnessed a ton of dead bodies having their own concert, and he was the only audience member, well except for myself, of course. I quietly walked out the establishment and headed home in the darkness.

———————

After a chaotic night, I was finally able to sleep. I couldn't remember how long I was asleep, but it felt like forever.

"Abella," I heard the soft echo throughout the room.

I turned my head as the cold breeze eased through my curls. Staring hard, I wondered why in the world was my bedroom window open. I had closed it before I went to sleep, as I always did. The breeze filled my room, forcing the long baby blue sheer curtain to sway back and forth in a beautiful motion.

My feet hit the cold wooden floor as I made my way over to the window. I blinked as I thought I saw something running through the dark field. I was no fool. Something was out there.

"Who's there?" I called out.

Blinking again, I noticed the grass had stopped moving. I stared at it for a few seconds, but it didn't move again. My mind was playing some sort of trick on me. With all the drama and everything I had been into over the last couple of weeks, I had become overly paranoid. For what reason, I had no clue. I was like untouchable, even the voodoo queen herself couldn't touch me, if she even exists. Perhaps she was just a myth to scare folks into not using so much of their power and gifts.

Over the past weeks, I had been seeing an incredible witch doctor who taught me very well. I learned my strengths and my weaknesses, and mostly everything else I needed to know. I heard the whispers again.

"Yes, I am Abella. I am here," I whispered back before hopping back into my bed.

I lay in the darkness and thought about Dylan, my Dylan, as I watched the shadows in my ceiling roam about and taunt one another. I started to laugh out of nowhere, and at that second, I realized that I was going crazy. It was probably too late for me to get help, even if I wanted some.

Chapter 20

Summer

Murphy burst through the door like a bat out of hell. I was in the kitchen preparing our dinner. I didn't expect him to be home so soon, he was supposed to be gone for a week, due to his work. But I didn't question it. I was more than excited to see him.

I turned around to see the mud tracked in the house. I hated when he brought all the dirt from his job home. He knew I hated the house to be all tracked up.

"Why didn't you take your shoes off at the door?" I asked as I stared down at the mess that he had just made.

He stood in front of me, shaking uncontrollably, unable to answer.

"What is wrong? Is everything okay?" I asked Murphy as I dropped the wooden spoon and raced to his aid.

I sat him down in the chair at the kitchen table. His eyes were big and wide, as if he'd seen a horrible sight. His palms were very sweaty, along with his body, which was hot as if he was overheated.

"Murphy, are you okay?" I asked again as I nudged him just a bit.

He began to mumble something. His mouth was moving so fast, I couldn't make out what he was saying. He stared at the wall and not once did he look at me.

"Did someone come visit you?" I asked.

He shook his head up and down. At that moment, I knew that someone had done something wrong to my husband. I was born into it. I knew better. To Murphy, this was all knew to him. He knew nothing about it, and I wanted him to never have any parts of it. This was the lifestyle that I tried my best to keep away from him.

I could easily undo what was done to him, if I knew exactly what it was. I had the gift of healing, a power I had never used before.

"Did someone touch you? Did you eat or drink anything? Who came to visit you?" I asked Murphy what seemed like a million and one questions.

He stared at the wall, not saying a word.

I got up and made him a cup of tea to calm him down a bit. Murphy had come home in a wreck, when I wanted to deliver to him the best news ever. After he drank his tea, I helped him upstairs to the bathroom, where I ran him a hot tub of water. I carefully helped him take his clothing off, and placed him into the tub.

As soon as he got in the tub, the soil from his feet turned the water black. I drained the water and re ran him clean bath water. He rested in the tub and pulled his knees to his chest. Tears sprang from his eyes. I felt so bad for him. I didn't want Murphy to know that I was a part of a world that involved so much magic, yet could be so evil.

I went into the bedroom and grabbed my bag that was hidden deep in my closet. When I went back to the bathroom, Murphy was in the tub rocking side to side.

"Was it Abella?" I asked him.

He nodded his head up and down. I shook my head; I couldn't believe the nerve of Abella. Something had to be done. If not, Abella might take my husband from me. I didn't know how far she would go, and I sure as heck didn't want to see it. She was my friend, or so I thought. But one thing I didn't take kindly to was someone messing with my husband.

"Murphy, you are going to be a dad!" I blurted out.

A smile came across his face as he reached his hand out and beckoned for me to come closer. I moved closer to him and he grabbed for my shirt. He lifted it up and softly rubbed across my belly.

Without warning, his touch became harsh and he started to squeeze my belly. "Get off me, Murphy!" I screamed, smacking his hand away from me. The possessed look on his face sent chills up my spine.

I grabbed his hands and squeezed them. At that second, I could see what had happened earlier that day at the funeral home.

"Damn you, Abella," I said as I walked out the bathroom.

It took three days and a lot of working and magic to heal Murphy. A part of me wanted to pay Abella a visit, yet I had no words for her. Instead, I decided to give her a taste of her own medicine.

One thing Abella didn't realize was that I had more gifts than she had, my powers were stronger than hers. Just because I refused to do the things she did, she'd underestimated me. If she wanted to play games, it was time to let the games begin.

Chapter 21

Abella

I couldn't take it any longer. My heart ached at the mere thought of Dylan cheating on me. Not my Dylan. I couldn't understand why and how we got here. My love for him was wildly growing out of control. I didn't know if the love was real or just superficial. Regardless, I just couldn't lose him, so I was forced to do what I had to do to keep my man, and to keep our love alive by any means. It was 'til death do us part, and I see it no other way. I thought back to what Summer had said the last time I saw her. She said what Dylan and I had was unreal. She spoke a curse onto us, onto our love. I was envious of her because she loved and had love back in return. She had what I truly wanted and needed.

The thought of them two made me sick. I eased out of the bed and grabbed my cell phone. Not one missed call. I pressed against the screen, scrolling to my favorites list and pressed my thumb on Dylan's name.

"Dylan, I just want to talk. I don't understand why you are doing this to me. Please call me," I said, damn near crying into the phone.

I stared at my reflection in the mirror. I couldn't believe I was allowing myself to fall apart because of this situation. The feelings were ill, and they were real. The heart wants what the heart wants, and there's no fighting against it.

After getting dressed, I sat and waited for the sun to go down. The doctor that I was seeing only liked to be seen after the sun went down. She was never seen in daylight. In fact, I'd never seen her in my life. Her muffled voice was all I'd ever heard. She would always be in the back room of the store. I had to talk to her through a door, and that's how she taught me, right through the door. Rumor had it that she didn't want to be seen because all the ugly things she had done in her life had turned on her, and she was just as ugly physically. That again, I couldn't vouch for. I've never ever seen her.

As I walked down the street to my destination, I must have called Dylan about a hundred times. I just wanted to hear his sweet voice. I wanted him to pick up the phone and tell me he needed space, which he wouldn't have gotten much of, but I would have given him some space. I just wanted to hear those words of reassurance that the two of us were still good, and that was all.

The thought of him brought hurt into my heart, anger into my body, nearly bringing tears to my eyes. A sense of relief overcame me as I stood in front of the double glass doors. "Sorry, Dylan, you will love me one way or another," I said to myself as I pushed my way through the doors.

"I want him to love me, love me the way I love him. I want our love to be forever," I said, as I stood outside the door waiting for an answer.

"You are back again, yet again you are back. And you'll be back again. He'll love you forever, but you must be careful what you ask for." She spoke in a soft muffled time. "Be careful of all the things you ask for," she said, as she slid the key to my happy love life underneath the door.

"Yeah, yeah, don't tell me what to do. Just make sure you continue to deliver what I need, and I will continue to pay you," I said and raced back to my house.

I couldn't get back to the house fast enough. Dylan wanted to act up, act as if he didn't care about me, even worse, as if he didn't love me any longer. In order to keep my man and to keep him under control at all times, I had to resort to a control spell. He would be mine forever, to do as I say, do as I please.

I unfolded the paper and read the contents. Then, I went and gathered all of the things that I needed to cast my voodoo control spell on Dylan. The paper stated that the spell had to be cast on a Thursday. I was so happy that today was Thursday.

A part of me felt that this was supposed to happen. I needed something that connected with Dylan to identify him, so I pulled out a picture of him, and to be on the safe side, his favorite shirt. He considered it his lucky shirt. Whenever he did something important, like a test for school or anything like that, he would wear his lucky shirt underneath his clothes. What personally connected Dylan more than his lucky shirt?

Following the instructions, I took a piece of paper and wrote Dylan's name on it five times, and folded it up six times. I was beyond excited. The smile that I wore on my face stated it all. I excitedly rubbed my palms together before I moved on to my next step. I took the paper and created a package, then I grabbed my twine to secure it. The package represented Dylan to the fullest.

I lit more candles, then closed my eyes as I sat Indian style and began to work my magic. "Queen, I come to you for help. I need my man, I love him more than I should love anyone. Yet, he doesn't love me back. Please help me not control him, but show him where his heart should be. Thank you."

When I was done, I was well satisfied. I began cleaning up my work and then patiently waited on my bed, staring at the ceiling. A vivid image of Dylan and a high yellow female came across my mind. It was crystal clear, as if I was staring at them, watching their every move. I could even smell the Dylan's scent. I jumped to my feet as tears ran down my face.

Anger, hurt, and all sorts of horrible thoughts ran through my head as I raced to Dylan's house.

Chapter 22

Abella

I couldn't believe that I had caught Dylan cheating on me red handed. Not able to handle him nor her the way I wanted to, I ended up running home and crying my heart out. I tried calling Dylan numerous times, but he didn't answer any of my calls. An hour later, I found myself back at his house. I was thinking about using my gifts. My broken heart had just wanted answers.

Summer's words struck me like a firing blade ripping right through my bare flesh. *Be careful, Abella, you are getting out of control. You are playing a dangerous game, and it all will come back to you even worse.*

Tears fell down my cheeks and ran down my black satin dress as I was pinned to the teal colored wall. My body felt as if it was paralyzed from the waist down. I couldn't feel my feet nor my legs. As much as I tried to move, I couldn't move at all. I stared at the body lying on the floor. The body belonging to the man who I love so much, the only man I ever loved.

"What did I do?" I said, barely above a whisper.

The question was what hell didn't I do? I had been in all sorts of devilment over the past couple years. Into any and everything. Overstepping my boundaries and taking my gifts for granted, overusing them and misusing them. I had been warned many times.

My heart frantically beat what felt like a million times per second. I gasped as I tried to catch my breath.

"Somebody, please help me," I began to cry.

My eyes grew bigger as they feasted on the large shadow that had risen above me. It hovered over Dylan. Then, I saw the familiarity of a set of beautiful eyes that I could never forget. I wondered for a second why she was there, and if she had come to save me. She was known to be the best at what she does … that is when she did what she did. Most of the time, she was cooped up in her home, far out on the bayou, away from everyone and everything. Just how she liked it. Distanced from the world.

"Aunt Aida, please, please help me," I squealed.

I never thought I would be so happy to see this witch. At that second, my life was in her hands. I depended on her desperately to get me some help, or better yet, save me herself.

"HAHAHA." She bellowed the most wicked and evil laugh I've ever heard. The laughter filled the house. Her shadow grew bigger and bigger. Then it disappeared as her laughter stopped. Paranoid, I searched the dark room with my eyes. In an instant, tons of candles lit the room up like it was the 4th of July. Just as abruptly as the candles came on, they went back out, plunging the room back into darkness.

I stared at the reflection in the doorframe as Aida appeared and disappeared. "I'm not afraid of you, you old witch"

Truthfully, I was afraid of her, afraid of what she was going to do to me. I'd heard so many rumors about her, but I would never mess with her. She was a lot older, more experienced, and of course, a lot wiser than I was.

"What do you want from me?" I yelled as loud as I could.

I searched around the room for Aida, who was nowhere to be found. The windows on the left side of the room starting to open and close. A breeze ran through the room, followed by a thick cloud of smoke.

I jumped as Aida followed the cloud of smoke. The wicked laughter filled the air again. Chills and goose bumps covered my body. I began to wiggle, trying to break free.

Aida's toes tapped against the ground lightly as she floated across the floor.

"He was my son," she cried out. "The only one that made it."

The tears running down her face were very visible. Never once had I seen this lady show any sort of emotion. She had to be hurt; she was never able to keep any of the children she'd tried to make. All of them died before birth. It was said that she had a curse on her when she was a little girl.

I stared at Dylan's lifeless body on the floor. I wanted him. I loved him with everything, but my control spell had backfired. I only came to Dylan's house to talk to him. I had many questions and needed answer. When I tried to walk away as Dylan became so aggressive, I accidentally stabbed him in the heart.

"I'm sorry, Dylan," I had cried. I cried in his arms as he stared me in my eyes and took his very last breath.

My mind went back to not being able to read Dylan. He was covered and protected by Aida, and that's the reason I was never able to read him. It was all starting to come clear and make perfect sense. He said his momma didn't like people of my kind. Aida used to always tell us we were people of a different kind.

My aunt had always told us that when she got closer to her due date with all of her children, she would disappear. We all went off the mere rumors of all her children being stillborn. She never denied it or admitted to it. We weren't allowed to her home or near her home. It all makes sense; maybe she was hiding Dylan from us, or perhaps he was one of the other children that she claimed she had lost. Maybe he had siblings still alive somewhere in this crazy world.

My heart raced with the fact of me falling in love with my very own flesh and blood. The sickening thought of me loving and being intimate with my first cousin brought vomit up from my core.

Vomit ran all down my black lace and satin dress. I closed my eyes as I tried to use one of my powers.

The power of freedom. All I wanted at that moment was freedom.

When I opened my eyes, I scanned my surroundings and noticed that I was in a graveyard. I stared at the tombstones that rested in front of me. Dylan's name was on the far right one, mine was next to his, then Summer's and Murphy's, Adele and everyone else I had done harm to. I was the cause of it all. All except Adele.

I never did any harm to her, but as for everyone else, I had harmed them and myself. I stared at the exit of the graveyard and began to make a run for it. I knew well enough that I could run, but I could never hide from what Aida, the voodoo queen, had put on me. I had no clue what she'd done to me.

I closed my eyes again and noticed that nothing was working. At that moment, I realized that I had been stripped of all of my gifts and everything that I knew. I thought about me being careful for what I asked for. As I was doing all of my dirty deeds, I never thought twice about the repercussions of my actions. Now it had all come back even worse.

Hearing lots of footsteps, I turned around and noticed dozens of little dolls racing toward me.

"Leave me alone!" I cried.

The dolls had the faces of Murphy, Dylan and Summer. They raced toward me as tears of blood dropped from their marble like eyes. I made it to the end of the graveyard and was greeted by Aida.

"What do you want? What do you want from me?" I cried.

I stared down at my feet and my arms, and noticed blood dripping down from them where I had been pierced.

"I want nothing from you. You have nothing to offer me," she said and walked away with her long black sheer dress dragging on the ground.

I turned around and saw the dolls getting closer. I tried to exit the graveyard, but for some reason, I couldn't leave. It was apparent. There was no way I was leaving there.

I ran back to where our graves were and stared into the empty tomb where my grave was supposed to be. Stuck in the ground was the same very knife that I used to accidentally kill the love of my life.

I grabbed the knife, stuck it deep into my heart, and fell right into a dark hole, where it was cold and lonely, lonelier than my life itself.

My chest heaved up and down as my heart began to faintly beat. 1 … 2 … 3 my heart then skipped a few beats.

"What are you doing?" I heard the voice say.

I blinked, forcing my eyes open, I noticed Summer standing over top of the hole.

"What are you doing? Are you okay?" she said with the most angelic smile.

Then, I saw her beckon for someone. Dylan appeared, looking ever so handsome, his smile was just as heart melting as the day we met.

"Baby, are you okay? Come out of that hole," Dylan said.

I tried to move, but I just couldn't. My heart heaved up and down as I fought to take another breath. "Summer," I softly said.

"Abella, what the hell are you doing? Are you having fun yet?" She spoke again with a devilish smile.

Murphy walked behind her and wrapped his arms around her, then he began rubbing her belly. A bit of jealously overcame me as I saw the protruding bump in her midsection. I always wanted a child. I wanted to be a momma … At that moment I realized that I had been tricked.

They all were amongst the living, and I now was close to sleeping with the ones who roamed all through the night. I learned that I had been duped, played at my own game. I was the loser in the end. It was beyond an illusion. It was fou magic!

"Until death do us part," I whispered as I took my last breath.

The End

Star City Publications Books

www.starcitypublications.com

Envy the Root of All Evil (Part 1)

Raven's Cravings

Momma I Ain't NO SAINT!

Gold Diggin' Honeys

Love On LockDown

Envy The Root Of All Evil (Part 2)

Pretty Money

Almighty Dolla (Anthology)

The Prodigal Son

Envy the Root Of All Evil (Part 3)

Promise Land

Ryder

Untamed And Deranged Mates

The Bentleys

Envy The Root Of All Evil (Part 4)

Hell Between My Thighs

The Streets Can Wait But My Love Wont

Recipes

SAUSAGE JAMBALAYA

2 pounds of smoked sausage
½ cup of oil
1 large onion (chopped)
2 stalks of celery (chopped)
1 medium bell pepper (chopped)
2 cups of uncooked rice
4 cups of water
Salt, black pepper and cayenne, to taste
½ cup of chopped green onions
½ cup of chopped parsley

1.Cut smoked sausage into four-inch links and boil in two quarts of water for 25 minutes. Pour out excess water and slice sausage into bite-sizes pieces.

2. Brown sausage in heavy skillet in cooking oil until well-browned.

3.Add onion, celery and bell pepper and cook until onion is transparent.

4.Add rice and water, along with seasonings. Cover and cook over low heat, stirring frequently. (if rice does not seem to be cooking thoroughly through the process, continue adding water in small amounts until cooked and no longer mushy, perhaps one hour.)

5.Add green onions and parsley just before serving.

Yield: 6-8 servings.

SHRIMP-STUFFED BELL PEPPERS

½ cup of chopped onions
¼ cup of chopped celery
2 tablespoons of butter
Salt, black pepper and cayenne pepper, to taste
1.2 cup of tomato sauce
2 cups of cooked rice
6 medium bell peppers
¼ cup of breadcrumbs
1 ½ pounds of shrimp, cooked, peeled and chopped (save 6 for garnish)

1.Sauté onions and celery in butter until onions are transparent, add salt, black pepper, cayenne pepper, and tomato sauce and simmer for about 6 minutes.

2.Add rice and shrimp and mix thoroughly.

3.Cut a thin slice rom stem end of bell peppers and remove seeds, drop shells into boiling water for 5 minutes and drain.

4.Fill bell peppers with shrimp stuffing and sprinkle top with bread crumbs, bake at 350 degrees for 30 minutes in a covered baking dish. Uncover and bake another 10minutes.

Yield: 6 servings.

LOUISIANA PEAR CAKE

½ cup of oleo, softened
1 cup of sugar
1 egg
1½ cups of flour
¼ teaspoon of salt
1 teaspoon of baking soda
½ teaspoon of cinnamon
1 teaspoon of vanilla
2 cups of grated raw pears
½ cup of chopped pecans

1. Mix oleo, sugar and egg together.

2. Sift flour, salt, soda and cinnamon together add to sugar and egg mixture.

3. Add vanilla, pears and nuts and mix well.

4. Pour into greased and floured backing dish or pan 8x8x2 inches.

5. Bake at 300 degrees for one hour, serve with whipped cream.

CAJUN SMOTHERED CHICKEN

1 chicken, cut into serving pieces
Salt, black pepper and cayenne pepper, to taste
½ cup of oil
1 pound of fresh pork sausage
3 large onions (chopped)
1 large bell pepper (chopped)
4 stalks of celery (chopped)
2 teaspoons of garlic powder
2 cups of water
½ cup of chopped green onion tops
½ cup of chopped parsley

1. Season chicken with salt, black pepper and cayenne pepper: brown chicken in hot oil in large heavy skillet and remove from skillet when brown.

2. Brown pork sausage in oil, remove from skillet and cut into 1-½ inch pieces.

3. Remove most of the oil from the skillet and add onion, bell pepper and celery: cook until onions are transparent.

4. Add pork sausage, chicken and garlic powder to skillet with onions; slowly add water, cover and simmer 30 to 40 minutes.

5. Add green onion tops of parsley just before serving; serve cooked rice.

CHICKEN FRICASSEE

1 hen (4 to 5 pounds), cut into serving pieces
Salt and cayenne pepper, to taste
6 tablespoons of oil
6 tablespoons of flour
2 large onions (chopped)
4 cups of hot water

1. Season hen with salt and cayenne pepper and brown in hot oil; remove hen from oil and add flour, stirring to make a dark brown roux.

2. Add onions and cook until they are transparent; return hen to the pot, add water and cook on low heat for about 2 hours or until hen is tender.

3. Serve over cooked rice or debone hen and serve in patty shells.

Yield: 6 servings

BATTER FRIED CRAWFISH TAILS

1 egg, beaten
¼ cup of evaporated milk
½ teaspoon of prepared mustard
¾ teaspoon of salt
¼ teaspoon of black pepper
¼ teaspoon of garlic powder
1 cup of flour
½ cup of corn meal
½ teaspoon of baking powder
1 pound of large, peeled crawfish tails
Oil for frying

1. In a bowl, beat egg; add milk, mustard, salt, pepper and garlic powder and mix well.

2. In another bowl, sift flour, cornmeal, and baking powder together and stir well.

3. Dip crawfish tails into the egg mixture one at a time; drain a little and dip into the flour mixture.

4. Drop in hot oil at 375 degrees and fry until golden brown; drain on paper towels.

Yield: 4 servings.

The Baltimore Crime Family

A Novel by Angel Williams

Prologue

Nina's heart beat erratically as she ran down the street. For the first time in over three decades of living, she feared for her life. Not just for her life, but for her children's lives as well. Her children were her world, her life, her everything. If there were a choice of death for either her or her family, she would make the deadly decision of giving up her life. But not without putting up a fight. A hell of a fight, at that.

As Nina ran down Edmonson Avenue, the slight hill gave her extra speed. Her short arms swung on the side of her as her sweat glands erupted and showered her face with hot sticky sweat. Today had to be the worst day to get jammed up. The sun beamed on her dark chocolate skin, throwing off more heat than she had bargained for. It was 105 degrees outside, and that day had been declared a 'Code Red'. The weatherman advised everyone to stay inside unless it was an emergency.

For Nina, when it came to money, she had to always get up, get out there, and get it by any means. She had five mouths to feed, and she didn't dare let them down. If she didn't get out there and grind, then she would be a failure to her children. They didn't eat unless she grinded. It was as simple as that.

Today marked exactly one year since her husband, Dylan, was taken from her by the murderous hands of some money hungry criminals.

Nina was only a few blocks away from her row home that was located on Gilmore Street. She made a sharp left and quickly peered behind her, only to see that her attackers were still on her tail. The shoes she had on had been left behind many blocks back. Now, the scorching hot ground burned her bare feet. Saving her life was on her mind, so she ignored the hot intense pain. Never did she see the man in front of her. She literally ran into his open, not so welcoming arms.

He towered over her 5'1" 135-pound body. "Going somewhere?" He smirked before sending a jab to Nina's sweaty, but still pretty face.

Although Nina's locks were scattered over the top of her head, and her face rained with sweat and screaming fear, she was still the epitome of beauty. She had the most beautiful chestnut brown eyes, dark smooth skin, high cheeks that were pierced with dimples on both sides, and a nice set of full lips. Her beauty was natural and undeniable.

Nina was instantly knocked off her feet. Lying on the ground pretending to be hurt, she decided that if she was going to die today, someone was going down with her.

The man bent down and spat in Nina's face. Before the spit landed on her, she jabbed him in the throat with an open hand.

"Ahhh!" He grunted in agony as he held his aching throat.

Nina jumped up and kicked him in the balls. Before he was even able to react, she pulled a switchblade from the back pocket of her Daisy Dukes and sliced his throat. No witnesses were there, just her, her attacker, and the other three men who were on her heels. Even if there was a witness, no one would dare snitch. Baltimore had zero tolerance for snitches. Like they say, snitches get stitches. In Baltimore, it was even worse. Snitches always landed in ditches.

When Nina made it to her front door, her youngest daughter, Amina, was out on the front steps playing with her Barbie dolls. Nina snatched her pride and joy up by one arm, and they rushed into the house.

"Get your brothers and hide. Now! Don't come out until I say so," Nina instructed her daughter.

Amina hugged her mother, who quickly pushed her away. It was time for war, and she didn't have time for the lovey dovey stuff. Besides, her children knew that she loved them all unconditionally.

Nina placed all three deadbolt locks on the steel front door.

"I love all of you. Me and your father love all of you," Nina yelled out to her kids, who were now in hiding.

The front door was safe and secured. Nina raced to the back door, but it was too late. Three intruders had bogarded their way into her residence.

Nina looked each of the men in their eyes. They weren't shit to her. Although she worried what they might do to her, she showed no fear. Her husband had taught her not to fear any woman or man, and if she did fear them, to never let the fear show. Showing fear meant that you were weak, and a weak one could be smelled miles away. If they were capable of doing any harm to her, she was just as capable of harming them.

She sized the men up, and knew she could take all three of them down on any given day. Except, today wasn't that day. They had guns, and hers were out of reach, due to her children. Nina quickly grabbed a butcher knife that was lying on the kitchen table and ran toward the dining room where she had an open space to fight.

"Fight me like a man. Put down the weapons," Nina said to her attackers. She stood tall with her chest out like a boss, filled with pride and confidence.

"Fight you like a man?" one of the attackers spoke. "Bitch, put that knife down and take your ass whipping like a woman!"

He handed his loaded firearm to another attacker. He was ready to make an example out of Nina's black ass. It was bad enough that he couldn't stand blacks, but a back talking one just made his skin crawl, giving him an irking feeling that he just couldn't explain nor handle.

He moved forward, closer to Nina. They were standing in the middle of the wooden floor as if it was a boxing ring. He charged toward Nina and she sent a jab to his throat, just like she did his buddy. Before he could make another move, she whipped the knife out and sliced his throat. Blood splattered everywhere like a loose faucet.

The other two onlookers gazed at the vicious woman with an evil stare. If she was anything like her nut case husband, they knew they would end up dead if they tried to fight her with no weapon.

Nina thought about her daughter, who had been missing for almost a year. It was a set rule in Baltimore. If a person went missing and wasn't found within 48 hours tops, most likely they were dead. She thought about the afterlife she would have with her daughter and her husband. The joy the three of them would have once they were reunited. It hurt her heart dearly the way she and Nya had separated. After a horrible fight, she'd never seen nor heard from her daughter again. Searches were put out, and were still going on for Nya. To this day, no one had heard anything or had any sort of information. Although she didn't want to think it, she knew deep down that her daughter was long gone.

The men decided not to take any chances. They had come for the money that she owed, but questioning her would have definitely cost them their lives.

One of the men raised his gun, which had a silencer on it, and aimed at Nina. He placed a bullet right between her eyes.

Nina's lifeless body fell to the ground, directly on top of the man she had just killed.

He walked up closer to Nina and placed another bullet directly in the middle of her skull, making sure that she was good and dead.

"Find my money, and find them little bastards. If I can't find my money, I want all five of them bastards dead!" He demanded to his partner in crime.

The man nodded and set off in search of the kids. He looked under every bed, in every closet, even in the hampers, and still found no kids and no money. He had to find one or the other, or his boss was going to be on his ass.

He walked the long halls of the house as the floors creaked.

45 days prior ...

Nina had no choice but to do what she knew best to keep a roof over her kids head and food in their bellies. She had been living off of Dylan's money until she spent the very last penny of it. Her kids grew, and it seemed like the older they got, the more it cost to take care of them. She couldn't dare go down to social services and apply for welfare. She was Nina Bentley, for Christ sake! Instead, she went to Dylan's father, begging and pleading for his help.

The first two times he turned her down. He didn't have any trust in her whatsoever. She was desperate. In his eyes, when someone was desperate, they would do anything. She was asking for a large amount of supply. Something that it took years, hard work, dedication and most importantly, loyalty, for him to give his own son.

Leroy offered Nina money. He didn't mind giving her a couple thousand dollars to keep a roof over his grandchildren's heads and food in their mouths. However, she insisted on the drugs, which she could quickly and easily flip, until she had enough saved up for her children.

Nina had desperately wanted to give up on life, be with her husband in paradise, but she couldn't dare do her children dirty like that. They needed her, and most importantly, depended on her.

Nina opened her wallet and noticed that all she had left to her name was a measly $23. She ordered her children two large pizzas and was left with a dollar to her name. After the pizza arrived, she hit the streets. Desperation led her to Leroy's house yet again.

The third time has to be a charm, Nina thought to herself as she knocked on Leroy's doublewide door.

"You're back, yet again. Do I have to get some sort of restraining order against you?" Leroy said as he opened the door.

He was joking, yet at the same time, he meant it. Nina was starting to become a fly in the air. Annoying and never going away. One look at Nina, and he could see the desperation all over her face.

"I don't know how my kids are going to eat. I won't be able to provide a roof over their heads. I wouldn't know what to do with a regular 9-5. Please help me. I'm begging you, Leroy, do it for the children and Dylan."

"Come on in," he huffed with a wicked grin pasted on his face.

"I can't believe this shit," Nina said to herself as she stood in the bathroom stripping down to her birthday suit.

Every bit of her felt guilty, filthy and trifling. All these years she held loyal to Dylan, and now here she was, the first time she ever betrayed him was with his father, for the sake of her kids. Before stepping back into the room, she gave herself a pep talk and made an apology to Dylan. Hoping when she met up with him again in the next lifetime, he would forgive and understand her.

Three hours of sexing later, Leroy was well satisfied. He sent Nina home with three bricks of pure cocaine to help her get on her feet. No matter how much sex she gave him, she wasn't getting anything else out of him. He didn't pity her one bit. He did it for his son, and that was it.

"You said you can get rid of it fast, I need my funds back in exactly thirty days. Anything later, I will need interest. Anything later than forty-five days, I'm sending for you, with no questions asked or any explanations given. I won't have any mercy on you." Leroy spoke.

Nina had no choice but to agree. She knew Leroy was getting over on her, asking her for a profit of $150,000 back off three bricks. But she couldn't object. She needed him and his cocaine. She knew she could break it down, cut it up, and make at least $400,000. It pissed Nina off that Leroy tried to carry her like some thirsty whore on the streets, when she was the mother of his grandchildren. The disrespect and humiliation lead her to the deadly decision of taking a few black diamonds that he had hidden in his bathroom. The combination was his late wife's birthday, which was the first thing that came to Nina's head.

After flipping the three bricks, Nina allowed greed to take over her and cloud her decisions and thoughts. She decided the hell with Leroy, and took the money and purchased weight of cocaine elsewhere.

She never once thought about the repercussions behind her decision. Never once thought that Leroy was cold-hearted, and had no love for her whatsoever. Her bad decisions cost her life.

Leroy gave Nina exactly 45 days before he sent the deadly hit out on her life. He told his soldiers not to touch the children. After all, they were his blood. Nina was only a Bentley by marriage, so she meant nothing to him. "Dead or alive. The money she has is yours," he told his hit man in charge before he gave him Nina's address.

"Oh, and please don't harm my grandchildren," he said with a smirk before lighting up a Cuban cigar.

All five of the children sat upstairs in the attic, their bodies filled with fear. All except for Amina. She had been through so much, and had seen and experienced more than an average child should see or experience. Gazing over at her brothers and sisters in the dark, hot attic, she could see all of their big bright eyes. Her heart weakened at the sight of them. They had just been reunited, and she vowed that she wouldn't let no one or nothing come between them. If she had to serve and protect them, she was going to do just that.

Peeping down out of the small crack, she saw the armed man walking down the hall. He was clueless that they were hiding in the attic just above him as he paced back and forth.

Amina closed her eyes and said a silent prayer. She didn't bother telling her siblings what she was about to do. This day was bound to present itself sooner or later. She couldn't help but snoop into her mother's business. The last time she checked Nina's wallet, Nina had next to nothing in it. On top of that, Amina had seen the cut off notices and eviction notices weeks ago. Then, all of a sudden, the notices stopped coming. Aminae was no fool. She knew her mother was doing something that could cost her life.

Amina's feet lightly tapped against the floor as she slid from the attic. Like a ninja, she crept up behind the armed man. He never heard her nor saw her coming. She sized the man up. He was somewhat scrawny, weighing no more than one hundred and fifty pounds. She didn't care if he was scrawny or a heavyweight; her life and her siblings' lives were in danger. The man was an intruder and had declared murder, which she wasn't going to allow.

She was now behind him, holding her breath so she wouldn't get caught breathing on his back. Without a sound, she wrapped her arms tightly around his neck, and threw her feet up in the air, landing on his back. She pulled her body back, with her legs still wrapped around his neck. His face changed colors as she squeezed the life out of him. One hard pull of her body, caused his back to snap. Another forced pull with her arms around his neck caused his neck to break. She jumped down and held him as his lifeless body fell to the floor.

Amina gazed at the man that lay on the wooden floor. At a young age, Amina had learned that her hands were her deadliest weapon. Her brother was a child soldier, killed at the tender age of sixteen. He had taught Amina everything she knew.

Amina crept down the halls to find the last intruder in their home. She found him in her parents' room, searching through the closet. Indeed, he had found their safe with all of her parents' life earnings in it. She didn't know why her mother didn't just pay up the money that she owed. It wasn't like she didn't have it. It just had to be her mother and her stubborn ways.

Amina grabbed the sword off her parents' wall. Her father used to call the sword his warrior sword. He had told all his children many stories about the sword, and how he had taken numerous lives with the sharp deadly weapon. The man was so busy trying to break the code on the safe that he never felt Amina's presence behind him.

"Yes!" he whispered. He had just broken the code of the safe. Breaking and entering was something he specialized in. Breaking the code didn't take too long or too much hard work for him.

His eyes widened and he licked his lips as he observed the contents of the safe. Black diamonds shined, along with stacks of money. He knew that cash was involved, but not as much as what was sitting in front of him. The first thought to his head was, Freedom at last. With this much money, he no longer had to stand down for anyone who considered themselves his boss. Now, he could become his own boss, or perhaps, Thee Boss.

Amina raised the sword.

The man turned around and stared into Amina's emotionless eyes. He didn't get the chance to react.

With all her force, she swung the sword back and slammed it against his head. His head immediately disconnected from his neck.

"Yuck!" Amina whined as blood splashed all over her face and clothing.

Amina couldn't stand to get dirty. That's why her preferred choice of weapon was her deadly hands.

Amina grabbed a duffel bag from the closet and stuffed it with the black diamonds and money. She then grabbed the sword and rushed out the room.

"Gigi, Mayhem, Dylan Jr., let's go now!" she yelled for her brothers.

Her siblings were ecstatic to hear their sister yelling for them. They all jumped from the attic and raced to her. Embracing her tightly and planting small kisses all over her face, they thanked her for saving their lives.

"Where's mama at?" Dylan Jr. questioned.

"Grab everything that you want to take, and let's get out of here," Amina instructed her siblings, ignoring Dylan Jr's question.

They all rushed to their rooms and grabbed their valuable possessions. Amina only grabbed pictures of her parents before she washed up and changed her clothing.

"We got to leave. I'm pretty sure there are others who will be coming back for us," Amina yelled.

They all followed Amina. As she walked down the steps, Amina knew that they would have to face their mother.

"Mama!" Dylan cried, kneeling down and cradling his mother. Her eyes were wide open.

Gigi leaned over, kissed Nina on the lips, and closed her eyes. "I love you, Mama," he whispered.

Amina grabbed Dylan by the hand and pulled him toward the back door. That moment would haunt all of them for the rest of their lives.

Just as the five of them made it out the back door, and were exiting the gate, they heard a loud boom. They all threw themselves on the ground, and looked up to see their house in flames.

"We gotta move quick. Sorry, Mama, I had to do it. If the house is burned down, they will think that we are all dead now," Gigi announced.

They jumped to their feet and ran down the alley, leaving everything they had behind.

Chapter 1

Daddy is Coming

Two years prior…

Dylan had made up his mind. He had two kids in Somalia that he desperately wanted to have with him. The once a week letters and every other night phone calls weren't cutting it anymore. He wanted his oldest son and youngest daughter to be with their father like the rest of his kids were. It wasn't fair to them at all that they weren't living the life they deserved.

Seventeen years ago, he went to Somalia on a wild goose chase. He was looking for a new drug that would take Baltimore by storm. With him being the only drug dealer in Baltimore with this drug, he would be a self-made millionaire in no time.

His first trip over to Somalia was a disastrous failure. Instead of finding his drugs, he spent hell of money on Somalian hookers. One in particular snatched his attention, and he shacked up with her for over two months, leaving his family in America on the edge. Before going back home, he found out that he was going to be a father. He made promises to his Somalian lover, but failed them all.

A few years later, he found out that he had a son. He made another trip to Somalia to see his son, who was then four years old. Yet again, he became attached to another female and got her pregnant as well. This time, he made promises and kept them.

Dylan went to his wife, Nina, and told him that he wanted his children in America with him.

"I don't blame you, Dylan. Honey, if you want your kids, then go and get them. We can provide a better life over here for them," Nina told her husband.

Dylan loved Nina so much. She always had his best interest at heart, loved him unconditionally, and most importantly, right or wrong, she always had his back. Despite him doing the ultimate no no and having kids on her, she forgave him after leaving him for only five months. Her heart belonged to him. He held the key to her heart, her life. She couldn't be without him for too long.

Getting his kids and having them live with him in America was the decision. A week later, Dylan made the trip over to Somalia. He had no problem getting his son, Gigi. He had no guardians. His mother had died three years before, and since then, he had been living on the streets. When Dylan located his son and heard his stories, he felt like less of a man. What man would have his child homeless? Dylan beat himself up over not knowing. Had he known, he would have done much better for his oldest son. He promised Gigi that as long as he lived, he wouldn't go without.

Picking up his daughter, Amina, was a totally different story. Dylan took a deep breath before stepping inside the raggedy shack that Amina and her mother lived in.

All the fucking money I been sending this bitch, and she still living like this? Dylan thought to himself, before entering the home.

Stepping foot in the house, Dylan was even more disgusted at the way this woman had his daughter living.

"Yanni, what in the hell have you been doing with all the money that I been sending you?" Dylan questioned.

Yanni ignored his question, turned to face him, and held her hand out.

Dylan stared into her cold greyish eyes. Her eyes told him that she didn't give a fuck about him standing there questioning her, neither did she give a damn about their daughter. He regretted ever lying down with such a cold-hearted woman. In his eyes, men were meant to be cold-hearted and uncaring, not women. She was a trifling excuse for a woman, and he wanted no parts of her.

"I came to get my daughter."

"Wha chu gut fa me?" Yanni spoke in her broken English.

In Dylan's eyes, his daughter was priceless. No amount of money in the world could buy her. But he had to do what was best for his child.

He went into his pocket and pulled out a wad of money. "Twenty-five thousand, and I don't ever want to hear from you again."

"Thirty thousand," Yanni countered.

Dylan shook his head, but reluctantly went into his pockets and pulled out another five thousand. The two of them had an agreement.

Just as the money was being exchanged, young Amina came running from the back room. She had been working on her flexibility for her acrobat practice that was scheduled for later that evening.

"Daddy!" Amina cooed, jumping up on her father, who she saw once a year, if that.

Dylan wrapped his muscular arms around Amina. He was well built, had the physique of an athlete. Squeezing her tightly, he planted kisses all over her coffee complected face. "I love you, baby girl," he said as he gazed into her eyes.

"I love chu too," Amina replied.

He brushed her hair down the side of her heart shaped face and stood there admiring her natural beauty.

Yanni was a whore with no cares in the world. When she first told Dylan that she was pregnant, he didn't believe a word she said. On the day of her delivery, he was there to witness if this child was his or not. Despite the mesmerizing sea green eyes that graced her face, he knew she was indeed a Bentley. If he had any doubts, her loud screams as she made an appearance into the world assured him that she was his child. Her screams and cries sent chills up and down his spine. Although he knew that Amina was his, he still questioned her green eyes.

"My father is Arab!" Yanni screamed.

Dylan remembered that she had once told him that. Still, he could never be too sure, so he ordered a DNA test on site. Weeks later, he was 99.9 % Amina's father.

Amina shifted all her weight from one foot to the other, wondering why her father was staring at her the way he was.

"It's time." Dylan told Amina.

He had promised her years ago that he was going to bring her home with him for good. This was a blessing to Amina. She had grown weary of her living situation, and Somalia was no longer the place where she wanted to be. The green eyed girl couldn't wait until she breathed some fresh American air.

Amina looked at her mama then back to her father. He shook his head, assuring her that he was dead serious. Amina rushed to her room and grabbed anything and everything that meant something to her, which wasn't much.

Dylan and Amina walked out the door hand and hand. Amina had a promising future with her father; with her mother, she had hopeless dreams and nothing more. Dylan was the proudest father on earth. Now, with all his children together, his family was complete. Neither of the two looked back, and had no plans to do so.

Yanni didn't care either. She was happy now that her daughter was gone. Her son was resting in peace, so she could downgrade to a smaller house, save more money, and have her own free will. Come as she pleased, travel and do whatever her heart desired. Dylan had come at the perfect time. She couldn't care less about Amina. She loved her daughter, of course, because she birthed her. However, at times, she couldn't stand being a mother.

Yanni sat at the small wooden table and counted her proceeds. Money was the root of all her evil. She would lie, steal and possibly kill when it came to money. To her, you couldn't breathe without money. Greed had taken over her body many years ago. When her scams and conniving no longer did her justice, she began to sacrifice her body for a hit of money. Throughout Somalia and London, she was known for being Miss Easy/Busy Body.

Amina got in the back of the doorless and topless Jeep Wrangler. Instead of getting in the front along with his driver, Dylan sat in the back between his oldest child, Gigi, and his daughter, Amina.

He wrapped his arms around both of his pride and joy.

"Father, I forgot something in the house." Amina spoke in her best American accent.

"Gone get what you have to get and hurry up, Amina. We have a flight to catch."

Amina quickly jumped out of the jeep and ran toward the house.

Inside, Yanni was at the table counting her money and daydreaming about all of the things she would buy. First thing tomorrow morning, she was going to go out and wine and dine herself. She was even thinking about taking her first trip to America to visit some of her long time family. Perhaps she would run into Dylan and threaten him that she was going to take her child back, so he could pay out even bigger. She had never seen so much money in her entire life. Now that she had $30,000 lying in front of her, she wanted even more. Her greed wouldn't allow her to just settle with the money she already had.

Amina crept up behind Yanni. Standing behind her, she disgustedly shook her head. It wasn't a secret that she hated Yanni with every fiber of her being. She never looked at Yanni as her mother. Yanni would abuse her mentally and physically, and sometimes, she wouldn't feed her or clothe her. Whenever Yanni pleased, she would do horrible things to Amina that she would have to deal with for the rest of her life.

Standing behind Yanni, Amina felt like she owed her father everything in the world for coming to save her. The more she pierced the back of Yanni's head with her eyes, the hotter her hatred burned in her belly. To make matters even worse, Yanni had betrayed the only person Amina loved. For years, Yanni had been hiding the ultimate secret, that she was infected with full-blown AIDS. Instead of telling anyone, she spread the deadly disease to others. It was a strong possibility that Dylan was infected with the disease as well.

Amina took her arms, locked her fingers together, and stood on her tippy toes as she stretched. Preparing to do the task that she'd been waiting many years to do, she slightly bent backwards, and her back made a light cracking noise.

"Amina?" Yanni turned around.

Amina didn't say a single word. She hopped on Yanni, locking her strong legs around her neck. Yanni's long fingernails were atrocious from not taking care of them for many years. They were now long, hard and a brownish color. She dug her nails deep into Amina's flesh as she fought for her life.

Amina gripped her legs tighter around Yanni's neck like a Python. Yanni still fought for her life. Amina ended her life quicker than she anticipated, by bending her body backwards. Her hands touched the ground. CRACK! Yanni's neck snapped, and the chair that Yanni was sitting in fell backwards and Amina's back hit the cement floor. Yanni's lifeless body fell on top of her, broken neck loosely swinging from side to side. Her eyes were wide open and coldly staring at Amina.

Amina crawled from under Yanni's body, got up, picked the money up from the table, and placed it in a bag. She walked out the door, again not looking back. Her past was in her past, and she was leaving it there for good, hopefully. Her mind was already made up. She would never return to Somalia for as long as she breathed.

On the plane, Gigi and Amina both fell asleep. Dylan, on the other hand, couldn't sleep at all. Sleep never came that easy for him. He seriously had a bad case of insomnia, and an even worse case of getting money. He was up constantly making money. There were times when he didn't sleep for days, due to his hustler ambition. While everyone was asleep, he was up thinking about money and more money. Always devoted to making his next move his very best move. Soon, he was going to have so much money that his best move was going to be his last move, landing him in riches.

Today was no different. He watched his children sleep while he plotted. Both of his children looked so peaceful. His heart raced with joyfulness. Finally, he could be there for his family and make them all happy. He could hardly wait to introduce them to Nina, their new mother, and the rest of their siblings. Back in Baltimore, he already had a block party arranged for them to take place the very next day. A welcome home present for the two of them, and a welcome to the family present from the rest of the children.

Dylan gazed at Amina, who had her knees pulled up to her chest. His foot kicked her bag, and out fell wads of money. Dylan recognized the money from earlier in the day. The same money that he gave to Yanni. He gazed at Amina again then back at the money. He laughed to himself at his cold-hearted daughter. She was most definitely a Bentley, without any doubt. He went into the pockets of his denim jeans and pulled out a small box. Inside, was a gold linked chain; a small medallion dressed in cut diamonds hung from it. The medallion read B.C.F., meaning two things, the Baltimore Crime Family, also known as the Bentley Crime Family.

The Bentleys were one of the most notorious families in Baltimore. They were largely credited with the massive amount of drugs in the city, and Baltimore's murder rate. Feared by many and tested by none, they'd rather be judged by twelve than carried by six. They knew they would never serve a severe amount of time behind bars, because they had majority of the police, people of higher power, and most importantly, the mayor on their payroll.

Dylan took the necklace out of the box and placed it around Amina's neck. Only the privileged who had proven their loyalty to the family was awarded one of these necklaces. Having the Bentley last name was beyond royalty. Carrying the name meant a lot. Their name was legendary, and was carried by legends throughout their family. Not only did their name mean power and money, it had a long line of great history behind it as well.

Dylan swooped the money up and placed it back in his pockets where it belonged. He knew that Amina had to kill her mother to get the money. As greedy as Yanni was, she wouldn't have given up a red cent without a fight. He then looked at the fresh cuts on Amina's legs, which assured him that Yanni had in fact put up a fight.

Dylan was a natural born killer, as well as a natural born hustler. His children all had his bloodline, and they too were natural born killers, whether they knew it or not. Deep down inside of them rested a bloodthirsty being that was not to be tested.

Out of his five children, Amina was the only one who had demonstrated her loyalty to him. In Dylan's thirty-six years of living, a little over a dozen of his friends and family had shown their loyalty. Amongst the ones that were still living, there were only approximately two dozen people who were privileged enough to grace their neck with the B.C.F medallion.

Amina was the youngest to receive one, and the only one of his children to have it. The rest of his children, he thought of as defenseless. He looked at them as punks. That all was going to change. He was going to train them and tame them to be the best, by any means.

Chapter 2

Fresh Start

Gigi got along with all the other siblings very well. He fit right in with the rest of them. Maybe it was because he was the oldest. Amina, on the other hand, had a harder time. As soon as the others saw the necklace that she wore, they instantly became jealous of her. Envying her for making their father proud before any of them had done so.

"Daddy, how is she wearing that necklace? What did she do to deserve it?" Mayhem questioned.

"She has proven her loyalty." Dylan spoke with a mouth full of food. "Gone head and tell them how you were awarded the necklace."

"I'd rather not speak on it," Amina replied.

Amina never intended to discuss the ones she murdered. Her motto was never kiss and tell, just as well as never kill and tell. Loose lips got you nowhere, and would most likely get you locked up. Only a dummy would commit a crime and go back to brag and boast about it.

Every day, the other kids would pick at and taunt Amina, making her feel very unwelcome. Gigi was no better; he never stood up for her. She thought he would, being that they came from the same place. That wasn't the case. The others outnumbered him, so he figured if he couldn't beat them, he would join them, and that he did. Still, it didn't bother Amina. If she had to be alone without her siblings, then so be it. All she needed was herself and her parents. No one else mattered.

One day, coming home from school, all five of the Bentley children were walking together.

"Aye yo, tell your father to stop selling that shit in our neighborhood. Allah is going to deal with him," one of the Muslim boys yelled out.

"Leave my father's name out of your mouth!" Mayhem spoke.

"Fuck your father!" the boy yelled.

None of the kids took it well when either of their parents were disrespected. Mayhem rushed over and uppercut the boy then two pieced him, knocking him straight out. His siblings joined in and began harshly punishing the boy for badmouthing their father. It took three fathers and some of the local drug dealers to break the fight up.

When they arrived home, word had already gotten back to their parents. Instead of them being disciplined, they were rewarded, mostly for standing up for the Bentley name, and for them all sticking together.

After that fight, the Bentleys learned to stick together and stand up for one another. They welcomed Amina into their family, and promised to never treat her differently again.

Chapter 3

Trust No Man

Dylan only trusted a few people. His circle was glove tight, and never did he want to invite newcomers into his tight circle. Trust was something that had to be earned with him, and trust, it wasn't an easy task. Once he didn't trust you, there was no turning back, matter fact, you'd be better off staying away from him, or always watching your back. Respect, you only got it from him if you respected yourself first, and him, of course.

Dylan had sensed some funny business had been going on behind his back within his crew. He didn't adore the sneaking around at all. Two things he hated were a rat and a backstabber. He had a big deal going down later on that day, so he drove his red Crown Victoria over to East Baltimore. He was on his way to pick up his right hand partner, Jamaican Redd to ride along, until he got a call from one of his many women.

"Dylan, daddy can you come give me a fix real quick? It's urgent that I see you." Tee cooed over the phone.

She lay across her bed, butterball naked. Her ample ass was tooted in the air. She slid two of her fingers her tight, horny canal. Slowly, she pulled her drenched fingers out, sucked them, and placed them back on her throbbing clitoris.

"Where you at?" Dylan asked, raising his left eyebrow.

Hearing the sound of her sucking her wet fingers, he envisioned her lying on her back, sliding her fingers in and out of her juiciness. At the sound of her voice, he instantly got a hard on. She always drove him physically and emotionally wild. Jamaican Redd was going to have to wait an extra few minutes, while he went to take care of some sexual business. When it came to sex, he was always fiending worse than a crack addict.

"Our spot, the Motel 6," Tee said, referring to the Motel 6 located on the west side, at Security Boulevard. Tee lived more than thirty minutes from this hotel, but to feel Dylan's long thick chocolate pole inside of her, she would drive a million miles.

Dylan's penis was brick hard, so hard that it was starting to cause pain. The only thing he could think of was being inside Tee. She was a few years older than he was, but she was an expert when it came to sex. She knew 101 ways and more to please him. With her, he was always satisfied and extremely pleased. Tee went above and beyond to make sure he was a happy camper once she was done with him.

Dylan weaved in out of traffic, turning corners and going approximately 90MPH or more, like a NASCAR racer. When he pulled up to the hotel, the car was barely in park before he jumped out, running to room number 69.

Tee always reserved room 69 for them. She thought it was kinky and fun to have the room number of their favorite sex position.

She stood in the doorway with nothing on but a pair of red stilettos. Her hands were on her thick hips, and her 38-D cup breasts stood alert. She was so horny that her juices ran between her thick thighs.

Dylan was in such a rush, he began taking his pants and shirt off before entering the room. He slammed the door behind him.

"Come to daddy." He called her to him while standing with nothing on but his socks.

Tee stuck out her tongue, cat walked over to him, laid on the bed, and spread her legs wide open. Dylan scooped her right breast up in one hand, gently massaging one while licking the other.

"Fuck foreplay. Let's get straight down to the dirty dirty," Tee seductively whispered in his ear while nibbling on it.

Dylan roughly threw her legs up in the air. Her feet were now touching the back of the wall. Her juices ran wild and his penis was throbbing extra hard. He carefully entered her and began to pound her insides out.

For the next thirty minutes, they fucked like two dogs in heat. They moved from the bed to the floor, to the dresser, and then ended up cumming in ecstasy back on the bed.

"I gotta go and pick your husband up. We gotta make moves," Dylan told Tee. He got up and began putting his clothes on.

"Uh huh. When you drop him off, come back and give me another dose of that good dick. I'll be waiting for you."

"I hear you, girl."

Dylan swore up and down that he had no weakness, but his weakness was really pussy. Pussy will get you set up, and even worse, pussy will get you killed. Those were the words of Dylan himself, but of course, he didn't practice what he was preaching and teaching.

An hour later, Dylan pulled up to Jamaican Redd's house. When it came to someone else's feelings, he didn't give a damn. He didn't even have the dignity to shower and erase Tee's scent off of him before hanging around her man.

He was the type to wait until a dude left the house, sneak in, fuck his girl, and then leave out like nothing occurred. Later, he would be smiling up in his face. If they asked questions or accused him of it, he would snap, and the outcome was never pretty.

Dylan had no remorse. Fuck your feelings is what he would always say. On the other hand, you'd better not try him or what was his. If you dared to look at his woman in a way that he thought was flirtatious, you would end up floating down someone's river with your head cut off.

Jamaican Redd strolled to the car wearing a pair of black cargo shorts with a red LRG top and a red bandanna tied on his head. His long dread locks flowed freely. They were black with fire red tips. His yellow skin glowed underneath the sun. He got his nickname, Jamaican Redd, for one, because he always wore red, and two, when he got angry, his light skin would turn red, which meant that he was boiling. If you knew best, you would get the hell out of dodge before he reacted.

He got into the car, and the smell of pussy quickly hit him in the face. His pussy at that!

"Damn, nigga, what, you been fucking all damn day?" Redd joked.

"Yeah, someone's wife," Dylan said, giving him dap.

"Your ass is always up to no good. Better be careful, my nig, I know niggas that done died over a piece of pussy."

"You gonna die one way or another, so why not die laying up in some good ole pussy?" Dylan expressed.

Redd shook his head at Dylan's foolishness. He didn't know whether to take his last statement serious or not. Dylan always joked. Sometimes he would seem to be joking, but he was actually drop dead serious.

Out making their runs, Dylan's cell phone was beeping off the hook, signaling that he was receiving text messages. He would look at the text messages and quickly delete them. Meanwhile, Tee was at the hotel assuming every position she could assume, and snapping pictures of them. She was waiting for him to come back and finish topping her off. The chick was beyond thirsty.

To stop the messages, Dylan powered his cell phone off.

"What's that all about? Is everything good?" Redd curiously asked.

"Shit's good, my nig. Just some bitch who can't get enough of me."

After making their runs, the two of them stopped by their spot that they called The Cage. The Cage was the spot where Dylan kept all of his products. Only certain members in the B.C.F family knew the location of The Cage.

Dylan and the crime family had their hands dipped in many different things, from drugs to prostitution rings, to boosters. One income wasn't enough for him. He wanted all the money.

He only trusted a few people to run his operations. His wife, Nina, his father and grandfather, and two of his brothers were his team. His younger sister ran the prostitution operation before she was killed in a crossfire. The empire that Dylan was running really originated from his grandfather, who would dip and dab here and there in the family business, but usually, he would sit back and just collect his profit.

Dylan had trained all of his children, hoping that sooner or later, they would be a part of the family. But in order to become a member, they had to prove to him that they were ready. Only they knew when that time was, which was when they were ready to become a man or a woman. His daughter, Amina, had already owned her part, and she was now a legit member of the crime family.

Dylan cruised around the outskirts of Baltimore and collected all of his funds. Most of his money came from the outskirts. The city was infected with the black plague, due to Dylan and his army of B.C.F that stood behind him.

Every first, fifteen and thirtieth of each month, the family would bag up twenty-five hundred $3 sample bags of dope and pass them out through the entire city for free. Fiends desperately waited for those particular dates just to get their free fix. When that date came around, the line formed so long, it was well over a four-hour wait at the trap house that gave out the samples.

Dylan considered giving his samples away as giving back to the community. That was his special charity. The fiends loved him for what he gave. Other than that, he gave back in positive ways. So children wouldn't see their parents lining up for their fix, across town, he gave out sneakers, school supplies, and $1 for every child that waited in line. The looks on the children's faces once given the free stuff was priceless. He wasn't such a bad person, he just always did what he could do. In fact, those on his good side regularly saw his heart of gold. Anyone on his bad side had to be prepared to meet their maker. He was far from a selfish being. Sometimes, his wife felt like he was always giving, and never received enough.

Chapter 4

Trained to Get the Job Done

Dylan loved all of his children to death. He would do anything for them. The kids and Nina were his world, but Amina in particular, he saw something else in. She had guts, she had a heart of steel, and she feared nothing. For all those reasons and then some, she was his favorite child. He looked at her as the golden child. Yet, he still loved all his children to death. Amina simply was different.

Amina was still a child, yet she was already trained to be deadly. In the country she was from, you were considered a woman at the age of twelve, and a man at the tender age of ten. In their country, war was a way of life, and getting prepared to fight in a deadly war was an everyday routine. Dylan couldn't wait to put her to work, although he didn't want her to become a woman at such a young age. His childhood was snatched away from him at the tender age of eleven. He was forced to be a man by his grandfather when he killed his first victim at the age of twelve. But all of that was way too late. Amina had already become a woman years ago at the age of nine, when Yanni snatched her childhood away from her.

Amina sat outside her parent's bedroom door, listening to her parents talk about a beef that her father had. Ever since Amina was a young child, she had adopted the bad habit of eavesdropping, listening through walls, picking up telephones and listening to peoples' private conversations. She was so much of an eavesdropper, that she had developed all sorts of techniques of listening through walls, looking through mail without opening it,etc.

In that instant, she decided she was going to do whatever it took to protect her father, and to protect her family. She stood at the door and listened to every detail. Her father had received word that a young member of their family had not only been stealing, but had become an informant for the west jump out boys (police). After Amina gathered the information, she began putting her plan of assassination to work.

She refused to let anyone snitch on her father and take him away from his family, most importantly, take him away from her.

A few days later, as she walked home from school, she saw Neal, the one her father had beef with, standing on the corner with a few of his homeboys. Amina gazed at Neal and flirtatiously licked her lips. She swayed her young hips from left to right as she strode down the block.

Neal and all of his homeboys had their eyes on her. They were all eighteen and older, and had no business gawking at a child the way they were, but like they say, a man is going to be a man.

"I'll be right back," Neal told his boys.

"Man, that's the boss' daughter. He would kill your ass if you even look at her wrong." One of his boys spoke up.

"Man, what he don't know won't hurt him. Besides, fuck him! I'ma do me, and ain't no one gonna stop me!" Neal barked.

Neal followed Amina down the block while looking at her ass.

Amina knew Neal was a dog, so she kept on walking, pretending that she didn't know he was behind her. She walked into an alley and Neal made the biggest mistake he could make in following behind her. Chasing pussy was a very dangerous game.

Amina turned around. "You following me?" she asked.

Neal rubbed both of his palms together while licking his lips.

She dropped her backpack to the ground. "You want this, yeah?" She teased while rubbing her hands up and down her body.

Neal was enticed by her young body. Not only was she very exotic looking with long locks and beautiful eyes, she was also smart, and far from comparable to the hood rats he was used to. She was in fact, a threat to the other girls in the neighborhood.

Amina lifted her shirt up above her head, showing off her B cup breasts. His mind went bizarre. Neal wasted no time grabbing her up and touching all over her body.

"Oh stop, Neal. You hurting me." Amina whined.

"Aww, shut up. Don't be playing no games with me, girl." Neal threw Amina on the ground and forced himself upon her.

"Stop!" Amina cried.

Amina was far from scared of Neal. She pretended to be weak, just to make Neal think he had the upper hand. Once he thought he had the upper hand in the situation, he let his guard down.

He roughly tried to rip off her pants. Amina could feel his pistol rubbing against her leg.

Neal's adrenaline began to race faster than his mind. He wanted Amina's fine ass right there and right now. He couldn't contain himself any longer. He was going to have her, one way or the other.

"If you going to make me do something that I don't want to do, at least let me get on top."

"Better for me. Gon' head and ride this dick, bitch."

The two of them switched positions. Amina placed herself on top of Neal. She then got on her knees and began removing her clothing.

"What you doing? Let's take this shit elsewhere before we get caught," Neal told Amina.

The two of them walked off to an abandoned building. Inside, were stringers and other crap that crack heads used to get high. When they couldn't find a place to take their blast, they would break into abandoned homes.

"Now, let's finish up where we left off." Neal smiled, rubbing his palms together.

With Amina being very cooperative with him, he knew down the line he wouldn't be able to catch any rape charges. He was Neal, Neal the man, and she was giving him exactly what he wanted.

Amina again started taking her clothes off. She abruptly stopped. "Neal, stop watching me, I'm nervous. I never did this before. Please turn around."

Neal hurriedly turned around and started removing his clothes. He stripped, and was ready to get down to the nitty gritty. Eager and overly anxious, he would do anything at that moment to have Amina. He envisioned himself sliding inside of her untainted canal.

Amina took her shirt off and wrapped it around both of her hands. The look of hunger lurked in her eyes. She was hungry to take the soul of Neal, who had been fucking her family over. You fuck with her family then you fucked with her, and in that case, you would be dealt with.

She made sure she had a tight grip on her shirt.

"Hurry up. I got shit to do," Neal said.

In the palm of his hands, he stroked his manhood. Amina had never seen a penis before, besides accidentally running in on one of her brothers, which was always a quick, sick glance.

Is that all he got? Amina thought to herself as she caught a glimpse at the size of Neal's small pecker. She wasn't a big fan of penis, but she thought she would have at least seen something a bit more exciting.

"Are you going to lay down or what?" Amina asked.

Neal's back was still facing her. He dropped to his knees in order to assume the position.

Amina immediately hopped on his back, wrapping her legs around his midsection. She took the shirt and wrapped it around his neck, squeezing it tightly. Neal fought back, throwing both of them to the ground.

Amina fell on her back, but never loosened her grip from around Neal's neck. In fact, her falling caused her to gain better access. While choking him, she took the back of her heel and harshly kicked him in the balls.

Neal grunted, but wasn't able to scream like the bitch he was.

It took Amina a little over six struggling minutes of choking Neal before he died.

"I thought that nigga was never gone die!" Amina quacked to herself.

She got up, cleaned herself, and then placed her shirt back on. With her backpack on her back, Amina ran through Neal's pockets, taking all of his belongings, and then left the house. Skipping down the street, she whistled, "Shame shame shame, I don't want to go to

Somalia no more more more," as Neal lay lifeless on the cold hard floor of an abandoned house.

Amina arrived home, went straight to her room, and did her homework as if nothing ever happened.

Later that night, Dylan walked into Amina's room to talk to her. Amina was lying on her back across her bed, searching through the cell phone that she had stolen from Neal. When she saw her father, she quickly tried to toss the cell phone.

"What's up, little one? What you just throw across the room?" Dylan questioned.

"Nothing, Daddy." Amina cooed.

Dylan excused her behavior. He always kept his eye on Amina. He was no fool, and knew she was always up to something. Mainly handling business and minding everyone else's business, especially his. He didn't mind one bit, he loved her and loved the way she tried to protect him.

"What do you want to do for your birthday?" he asked.

"My birthday?" Amina echoed.

"Yeah, your birthday, silly girl." Dylan began to tickle Amina until she almost pissed herself.

Although Amina was forced to be a woman at a young age, she still had so many childish ways about her, and loved to show off her inner child.

"Oh, Daddy, I forgot. Stop Daddy, I forgot. Daddy. Stop, I'ma pee myself." Amina giggled.

She had been so busy walking around the house eavesdropping and trying to protect her family that she had forgotten all about her birthday.

"I just want to spend the whole day with just you and me, Daddy."

"You the birthday girl, whatever you want can be done." Dylan told her.

"In that case, I want a horse for my birthday too."

"A horse?"

"Yes, a horse, Daddy. I love horses."

Amina loved horses. The closest she got to a horse was seeing one in a book or on television. She always pictured herself with a cowgirl hat on, riding off on a horse into the sunset.

"That can be arranged too. But we can't keep it in the city, it will have to be kept at your grandfather's house. But if that's what you want, I promise I will get it for you."

The next day after school, Amina patiently waited on the front stoop for her father to arrive. At first, she just wanted it to be her and her father, but not to be selfish, she decided to invite Nina and all of her siblings.

This would be her first birthday that she spent with her father and her family, actually, the first birthday that she ever celebrated. On her birthdays back home, Yanni would ignore her, never acknowledging that it was her birthday. She didn't get a peck on the cheek, no happy birthday, not a damn thing.

On the day of her birthday, Amina was super amped. She paced up and down the street as she waited for her father to arrive. Her hair was in a high tight ponytail, and her ends were curled. She wore a pair of pearl earrings, with a matching necklace set that Nina had purchased for her birthday, along with a powder blue baby doll dress and a pair of white sandals. Her overall look was adorable.

"He should be here by now, Ma, it's my birthday." Amina cried to Nina.

"I called him dozens of times. Don't worry, honey, he will be here any minute."

Nina was worried herself, but she didn't allow it to show. She kept a smile on her face, assuring Amina and the children that their father was just a little behind schedule.

Three hours later, Amina and Nya were still waiting on the front stoops for their father to arrive. They were excited about going out and celebrating Amina's birthday.

"Come on in, y'all. Mama said lets open up your gifts, Amina, while we wait for Daddy," Mayhem called out.

"I don't wanna. I'm waiting for Daddy to come home," Amina yelled.

The sun had gone down, and now the city was filled with darkness. Amina still hadn't gotten up from the stoop. She envisioned that any second she would see her father galloping down the street on her all white bushy haired horse.

"Come inside," Nina stepped outside and told Nya and Amina.

"I knew that nigga was bluffing. Bluffing ass nigga." Nya huffed as she got up. Nya knew her daddy was full of all sorts of surprises lately. She rarely saw him and knew he was out on the streets up to no good.

"Child, you better watch your mouth and stop bad mouthing your father before I knock your teeth down your throat," Nina threatened.

Nya rolled her eyes and strolled into the house. Nya was two years older than Amina, and didn't mind expressing whatever was on her mind. She said what she wanted to say, and when she wanted to say it. Her loose lips were her worst enemy.

"Just because your ass look grown and wanna act grown, that shit don't cut with me," Nina yelled.

"Woman shut up and stop barking all the damn time." Nya talked back.

Nina was frustrated that Dylan wasn't answering her calls. Nya talking back to her made matters even worse. One thing she didn't tolerate was a child back mouthing her.

She ran behind Nya, snatched her up by her long ponytail, and pinned her against the wall.

"What I tell you, little girl?" Nina yelled.

"Chill out and back off me." Nya sucked her teeth.

"You trying to be cute? You think this shit is a game? What did I tell you, little girl?" Nina smacked Nya in the face.

"If I'ma talk back, I better be able to back it up." Nya recited.

"You damn right. Now, Tough Tony, meet me in the fucking backyard. We gonna go toe to toe."

Nya didn't have any objection. She had no choice. Nina dragged her daughter to the backyard by her hair.

Nina didn't baby any of her children. She showed them all tough love, and if one disrespected her, she showed no mercy. The tough love she showed them would be better for them in the long run.

"All of y'all get y'all asses out here now!" Nina yelled.

The children stopped what they were doing and rushed to the backyard, even Amina. None of them dared talk back to Nina; they knew she was no joke. All except for Nya, with her young hot ass. She was the only one who didn't take their mother serious.

They all gathered outside. Nina stood on the right side of the yard, and Nya stood on the opposite side.

"If I beat this little bastard too bad, break the shit up," Nina told Gigi.

"Uh huh, you wish." Nya continued to pop her gums, making Nina even madder. She wished that sometimes her daughter would just shut up. She knew one day her mouth was going to write a check that she couldn't cash, and none of her siblings nor Nina would be around to protect her.

They were all too familiar with what was about to go down. They had all been in this situation. For most of them, it only took one time in the ring with their parents to learn how to keep their mouths shut. It took about five good knockouts for Mayhem. Nya, no matter how much she was knocked out, she still didn't learn how to keep her trap shut.

Mayhem rushed back in the house and reappeared with two sets of boxing gloves. He tossed a set to Nina and the other to Nya.

"Why we need the gloves? I'm used to this shit. Fight me like I'm a typical bitch in the street," Nya dared her mother.

"That's how you want it, huh?"

"Yup."

Nina began to take her gloves off. Nya wanted to fight dirty, so that's exactly what she was going to get.

Nya unexpectedly charged her mother, throwing wild windmill punches and kicks.

"If I beat this little bastard too bad, break the shit up," Nya mocked.

The two of them tossed each other around. Nya tried her best, but she was fighting a losing battle. Nina was much quicker and way stronger.

Nina had blacked out, and she'd forgotten that the girl she was fighting was her daughter. She picked up a Corona bottle that was lying around in the backyard and broke it upside Nya's head.

Nya refused to give up, even though her head was now dripping with blood.

"Bitch, you gon' have to kill me," Nya huffed, out of breath.

"May the best woman live," Nina said and wickedly laughed.

Neighbors who had heard all the commotion rushed to their windows and backyards to get a glimpse at what was going on. Some watched with astonished looks on their faces, while others egged the fight on.

"Beat her ass. She's fucking your man." One nosey ignorant bystander yelled.

"What? Girl, shut up! That's her fucking daughter." Amina yelled at the girl who was making statements about something she obviously knew nothing about.

Nya was most definitely giving Nina a run for her money. By constantly being in the ring with her mother, she had become much stronger and more hip to her mother's moves.

Nina threw a left punch, directing it toward Nya's face.

Nya quickly dodged the punch. Nina threw another, and Nya ducked again, missing the punch by seconds. She lifted her leg up to kick, and Nya grabbed it and pulled it so hard that Nina landed on her ass. She quickly got back up and threw punches again.

A left connected to Nya's jaw, and the ones that were close enough could hear the bones in Nya's jaw breaking.

"Ahhh." Nya screamed in agony.

"Give up." Nina yelled.

"Never! I'm my father's child!"

Seeing enough bloodshed from the two of them, Gigi quickly grabbed his mother while Mayhem and Amina grabbed Nya.

"Enough!" Gigi yelled. "Did y'all prove a point yet?"

"I wasn't trying to prove shit," Nya screeched.

"Trying to fight me like I was one of your little girlfriends, you act like you was trying to prove something. You going to learn, respect me or get dealt with. I'm no friend of yours. I'm your fucking mother."

"Respect to get respect," Nya said with a smirk.

Nina stormed off. "Child, please, you gets no respect from me. When your father comes home, I'ma make sure he deals with your ass. I swear, if I have to put my hands on you again, I'ma be burying my own damn child!"

"Woman, your man is probably out with a younger, way more fly chick, getting his grove on. You don't know? He don't want your old played out baby making ass. You're old news, boo."

Those words stung Nina like a hive of bees. She knew that her man creeped, but to hear it from her daughter was something else. If looks could kill, Nya would have been dead. Nina stared Nya deep into her eyes, giving her an evil look that caused chills and goose bumps to run through her.

She knew in that moment, that the relationship she and her daughter had would never be the same. She held that even stare for a pregnant minute.

KNOCK! KNOCK!

Amina took her eyes off her mother and her sister. She was filled with excitement as she rushed to the front door.

"Daddy, did you forget your key?" Amina asked while opening the door.

Standing in front of her were two uniformed men.

Amina's heart instantly sank to the pits of her stomach. She'd been having his bad feeling all day, now she knew her feeling was about to be confirmed.

"Yes?" Amina swallowed.

"Hello, my dear. Is your mother home?" one of the men asked.

"I can help you. What do you want?" Amina questioned with her arms folded across her chest.

"I prefer if we spoke with your mother, young lady."

"Ma!" Amina yelled.

Nina came to the door. She could barely get past Amina, who blocked the entrance.

"Girl, move and go play with your baby dolls or something," Nina said. All the commotion going on was working her last nerve.

"What y'all muthafuckas want? Showing up at my damn house at midnight," Nina snapped with her hands on her hips.

The detectives really couldn't stand the Bentley family. All the dirt they'd been doing, all the crime. They still weren't able to convict them on anything so far. The crime family always carefully cleaned up behind themselves, leaving no evidence behind.

Today, neither of them had any sympathy for the family, but they had to play the part in order to deliver their message.

"Who do I have the pleasure of speaking with?" the detectives asked.

"Nina. Y'all fools know who I am." Nina shook her head from left to right.

"Sorry, Mrs. Bentley, to be knocking at your door this late. There has been a terrible accident involving your husband, Dylan—"

"Shut up! Shut up! Shut the fuck up! Where is my husband?" Nina cried.

"Mrs. Bentley, like I was saying—"

"Is my daddy dead?" Amina interjected with a face full of tears. She had the feeling, and now she just needed confirmation.

The look the men gave Amina confirmed that Dylan was in fact, no longer amongst the living.

"No, no, no. Not Daddy. He promised that he would be back to celebrate my birthday with me. This is the worst birthday I ever had. I want my daddy," Amina selfishly cried.

Amina loved had father dearly. Yet, sometimes her selfish ways could get the best of her. She was looking forward to celebrating her birthday with her father for the first time in her life.

"Oh God. It's going to be okay." Nina was no longer able to hold her tears. "What happened to my husband? Tell me what happened. I need to know," Nina begged.

The police informed Nina that Dylan had been shot in the head twice; his body was stuffed in the trunk of his car, which they found on fire. The fire department was just able to put the fire out and save what was left of his corpse.

Nearly a mile down the street, they found another body lying on the side of the road headless. The headless body was unidentified, and the head has yet to be found.

Nina slid down the wall, pressing her knees against her chest. The hurt look on her face caused the detectives' cold hearts to ache for a few seconds. Nina covered her face with her hands, allowing her tears of pain to escape from her sorrowful eyes.

"AHHHHH! Not my husband! Not my husband!" Nina cried in pain, while banging her fist against the wall.

At that second, a piece of her heart died. A big chunk, big enough for her to declare herself dead. Without Dylan, she felt worthless, she felt like nothing.

The other children heard the commotion and came running into the house. 512 Gilmore Street was filled with aching souls. That night, no one was able to rest easy or have a clear mind. How could they? The man of the house was no longer there to serve and protect his family...

Nina ran her a bath filled with boiling hot water. She soaked for hours, trying to escape the pain.

Note: This is just a sample of The Baltimore Crime Family. Full Novel can be purchased on Amazon.com*